CHRISTMAS

WITH THE

BIKER

CASSIE ALEXANDRA

ONE

GRAHAM

NORMALLY, I'M NOT a violent guy and am pretty level-headed. For the most part.

But everyone has a breaking point; mine came on Christmas Eve, around two o'clock in the afternoon. It was totally unexpected and landed my ass in jail.

Worth it?

Hell, yeah.

The day actually started out pretty fucking fantastic. I'd shown up early for work—I'm a master electrician—to complete a job my company had been commissioned for, which was a newly constructed hotel. We finished before eleven a.m. and not only did I receive a nice, fat Christmas bonus, but also found out I'd won two airline tickets in a raffle contest I'd forgotten all about. So I was on top of the world and feeling like anything was possible, which was why I stopped at the jeweler on the way home from work. My girl and I had been dating for over two years, and I'd been thinking about proposing to her. She was beautiful, and in fact looked a lot like a young Demi Moore. Although neither of us had talked about marriage, I knew I wanted her to stay in my life, and a ring would at least make my intentions clear.

Anyway, after looking at several engagement rings, I purchased one I thought she'd love and had it wrapped in shiny red Christmas paper.

"Bonnie is going to love it," the saleswoman promised, handing me the small package with a tiny white bow.

Smiling, I thanked her and wished her a "Merry Christmas."

"You too, Graham."

As I walked out the front door of the jewelry store, I found myself whistling to the Christmas music playing. I stuffed a twenty-dollar bill into the Salvation Army bucket.

The man dressed as Santa Claus and jingling a bell, smiled brightly at me. "Thank you, young man. Have a Merry Christmas!"

"You, too," I said, grinning back. "Best time of the year. Except for the snow."

"The snow isn't so bad," he said, glancing up toward the thick, fluffy flakes that were falling. "To be honest, I can't imagine *not* having a white Christmas."

He was right, but… I was missing my Hog. I hadn't had it out since October and wouldn't see it until March or April. It was one reason I'd been putting money away for a snowmobile. Not exactly the same thing, but it was still as fun as shit. This money was now going toward the engagement ring, but

4

I didn't care. I was in the giving spirit and wanted to put a smile on Bonnie's face.

We chatted for a couple more seconds and then I went home to surprise the woman I loved. Turned out, the surprise was on me.

BONNIE HAD MOVED in with me two months prior. She worked out of our apartment selling bath-bombs, shower gel, and other perfumey shit on Etsy. It was now taking up most of our closet space and was a little irritating, but when you love someone, you learn not to sweat the small stuff.

As I walked in the door, I was still flying high and had no idea what was about to unfold. Not until I walked into the bedroom and all hell broke loose.

"What the actual *fuck*?" I gasped, seeing my neighbor—a piece of shit drug dealer—balls-deep inside Bonnie. If that wasn't bad enough, he shot his load as our eyes met.

"Graham!" Bonnie squealed, trying to cover herself with the sheet. "Oh, my God. What are you doing here?"

Shock turned to rage, especially when I saw Seth's jizz on the mattress. My fucking mattress that I'd paid three thousand dollars for because Bonnie couldn't live without it.

"I fucking live here, that's what I'm doing here!" I hollered.

"Hey," Seth said, scrambling to find his clothing. "Sorry, man. This just kind of happened. I gave her a sample of some ecstasy and ended up taking some, too. Things got out of hand, but it wasn't planned. Right, Bonnie?"

"Of course not," she said, her eyes filling with tears. "It was a mistake."

Seth pulled on his boxers. "Seriously, this shit is really powerful. The best I've ever sold. You should try some, bro. Or maybe some weed to calm you down. I've got a joint with your name on it. No charge, of course."

"Is that right, *bro*?" I said angrily. The next thing I knew, I was on top of Seth, beating him to a bloody pulp. It wasn't until Bonnie screamed that the cops were on their way that I came to my senses and pulled myself off of him.

"Graham," sobbed Bonnie, trying to touch me. "I'm sorry. I didn't know this was going to happen. You have to believe me."

"But it did." I snaked my arm away from her. "Pack up your shit and get the fuck out of my house," I growled before storming out of the room.

UNFORTUNATELY, THE COPS showed up and hauled me to jail on assault and battery charges. Apparently, one of the other tenants in my apartment building had called it in, putting the finishing touches on a most memorable holiday. I spent the next two days in jail, and was released the day after Christmas when someone made my bail. Interestingly enough, he was a stranger. Or so, I thought.

"Do I know you?" I asked the dark-haired man waiting for me in the lobby of the station.

"Not yet," he said, staring at me with interest. He held out his hand. "The name is Jordan Steele."

I shook his hand. "Graham Dodge. Why did you bail me out?"

"Because that's what family does, apparently," he said with a smirk.

His words made no sense. "Family?" I repeated, taking a step back. "I think you have the wrong guy. I don't have any family. Not living, at least."

Jordan reached into his coat pocket and pulled out an envelope. "Apparently you do. Read this."

I took it from him and opened up the letter.

Dear Slammer,

I've done some terrible things in my life and I'm trying to work through them. Thankfully, Jordan and Trevor have found each other and I hope that one day they'll forgive me. That being said, I hope you'll help me find my other son. Although I have a lot of regrets, I know leaving him in the church was the right thing to do. I was a mess, and all I cared about was getting high. I'm ashamed for so many things, and I'm trying to set things right, which is why I need you to help me locate him. Even if he doesn't want to have anything to do with me, he has two brothers and they'll want to know about him. In time, I hope I can face all three of them and ask for forgiveness. Drugs have ruined our lives and I have nobody but myself to blame.

The letter went on to explain where exactly she'd left her baby and when. It was signed by someone named Mavis.

"What does this have to do with me?" I asked Jordan.

"Both Slammer and Mavis are deceased, but Slammer's widow gave me this letter a few days ago. After doing some research, I found out the child she left at the church was you."

I stared at him in disbelief. "What? I don't think so."

"You were adopted, right?"

"Yeah, but they'd never mentioned anything about someone leaving me at a church."

"An administrator at Saint Michael's, the church you were left at, said you were given to an adoption agency and went to a home right away. Your adoptive parents are named Jack and Emily Dodge, right?"

"They were," I said, my heart heavy as I thought of the couple who'd raised me. Unfortunately, both had died after I'd graduated from high school. The only father I'd ever known, Jack, had been everything I could have asked for in a parent. Supportive, loving, and stern enough to keep me out of jail, even though I'd sometimes hung out with a rough crowd. Unfortunately, he'd smoked like a chimney and died of lung cancer.

Then there'd been my mother, Emily. She'd spoiled the hell out of me, which probably made me kind of an asshole, admittedly. She died a couple years after Jack, from a brain aneurism. Their deaths had been hard on me and Bonnie had been my salvation. Her betrayal was such a blow. It felt like someone else close to me had died, only this time... I didn't have anyone to help me through my grief.

"That's what I thought. If you check your adoption records, you'll find that Saint Michael's released you to them twenty-seven years ago."

"How do you know all this?"

He smirked. "I have my ways."

"What does this have to do with you?" I asked and then remembered the name in the letter. Jordan.

His lips twitched. "Apparently, I'm one of your older brothers."

A flood of emotions rushed through me. It was hard to believe what he was saying was true. "You sure about this?"

He shrugged. "We can take a DNA test."

So, in other words, this guy wasn't totally convinced yet either.

JORDAN STUDIED THE man next to him and he had to admit, he had some of Trevor's mannerisms. Like the way he held his head to the side when he talked, and the smile. They definitely had the same mouth and chin. As far as Graham's other features, his jet-black hair and darker skin tone reminded him a little of his own, which he'd inherited from his old man, Acid.

What if he was Acid's?

If that were the case, he couldn't exactly blame Mavis for trying to keep her pregnancy a secret from the bastard. He would have fought tooth-and-nail for Graham. For his *property*. Acid had been a homicidal maniac who'd taken pleasure in torturing anyone unable to defend themselves. Jordan still had scars, both physically and emotionally, from living with the scumbag.

"So, where do you guys live?" Graham asked as they began to walk.

"Jensen," he replied, which wasn't too far from Davenport, where he'd learned Graham lived. "By the way, Trevor is a member of the Gold Vipers. He's the V.P."

Graham stopped abruptly, a shocked look on his face. "You're kidding me? Ya know what? I think we've met before."

"Oh yeah?"

"Yeah. Just briefly," he said, a funny smile on his face. "At Sal's. I also met Tank there a couple of times. He and his wife Raina own that bar, right?"

7

"Yep."

"Small world," Graham said. "So, are you a member of the Gold Vipers as well? I noticed you're not wearing any of their club patches."

"Nope. It's not my thing."

"Why not?"

"I prefer solitude. And privacy."

Getting the point, Graham nodded and said no more.

When they got into Jordan's SUV, he asked Graham if he'd like to stop home or go straight to the clubhouse.

"The Gold Vipers' clubhouse?" he asked, surprised.

"Yeah. They're throwing you a party. It's supposed to be a surprise, but if I were in your shoes, I'd want to know about it first."

"You're shitting me?" Graham said in disbelief. "The Gold Vipers are throwing *me* a party?"

"Yeah. Get used to it. Trevor's accepted you into the family already, which means his club brothers are willing to as well."

"Wow, that's heavy," he replied, looking thoughtful. "What kind of party are we talking?"

Jordan smirked. "Since I ruined the surprise already, I'll let you see for yourself."

TWO

CHLOE

"CHLOE, ARE YOU okay?" Jessica asked softly. She'd caught me crying in one of the supply room at St. Peter's Hospital in Jensen. I was a new nurse in the Children's Cancer Unit and had just watched one of our patients die in his father's arms. Theo, a twelve-year-old boy with Leukemia, had been such a sweet kid and I'd grown attached to him in the last few weeks. Watching him die had been so heartbreaking that I'd almost walked out of the hospital.

Embarrassed she'd caught me crying, I cleared my throat and forced a smile to my face. "I'm okay. It was just so hard seeing Theo go," I replied, dabbing at the tears under my eyelashes with a tissue. "I thought I was going to handle it, but…" I smiled bitterly. "I guess not."

"You handled it perfectly," Jessica replied, touching my shoulder. "You were there for Theo when he needed you the most. When his *family* needed you the most. As far as this goes," she smiled sadly at my wet face, "it's okay to cry. You're a warm and caring person. If you weren't affected by something like this, we wouldn't want you here."

"How do you do it?" I asked. I knew she'd been working there for the last year and the woman not only always had a smile on her face, but she was so good with the children. Of course, she was a mother herself and that probably helped. "How do you deal with it when you lose someone you start caring about?"

"It's hard, but these kids are worth every bit the suffering and the tears. Whether they walk out of here or not, I do what I can to try and make their stay as comfortable as possible. Yes, I go home and cry all the time, but when one of them goes into remission or becomes cancer-free, it's the best feeling in the world to watch happen," she said, smiling.

I let out a ragged sigh. "I thought I knew what I was getting myself into. I just don't know if I'm as strong as you are at dealing with this."

Jessica's eyes bored into mine. "You're stronger than you realize. You did the best you could and made Theo's stay here better than it would have been if you weren't around. You're great with the kids, Chloe. You really are."

I smiled in gratitude. "Thank you."

"You don't need to thank me," she replied. "I'm only pointing out what you can't see at the moment."

The truth was, I knew I was good with people and truly enjoyed working with them. It was why I'd gone into nursing. Losing them, especially children, was something I knew would happen, but hadn't been prepared for.

"You know what you need? A party. Something to take your mind off this for a while. Your shift is over now, right?"

"Yes," I replied, staring at her in surprise. "A party?"

Jessica nodded. "It's actually a fundraiser, but you don't have to feel obligated to give anything. My stepbrother's club is sponsoring it, and knowing them, they'll raise more than enough money. I just want to stop in for one drink and I thought you might want to go with me. It might take your mind off of things for a while."

I had to admit, a drink sounded good and I was all for fundraisers. "Sure. I'd like that."

"Great. I'll pick you up at your place. Text me your address."

"Sure. Uh, so is this fundraiser formal or informal?" I asked, wondering how I should dress.

Jessica chuckled. "Informal. *Very* informal."

AN HOUR LATER, I stepped out of the shower and slipped into a pair of black jeans and a green fuzzy sweater. I quickly dried my blonde hair, pulled it up into a bun, and then took it back down. I hadn't gone out for a long time and it was time to relax and enjoy myself. Even if it was for just one drink, I really needed to unwind in every possible way.

"Wow, look at you," my roommate Kai said when I walked into the living room. He eyed me up and down and nodded in approval. "Don't tell me… you finally have a date?"

"Finally? Thanks a lot," I said dryly and then told him about the fundraiser.

"Ah. Well, I guess it's better than just sitting around here and watching reruns of *Game of Thrones* over-and-over, as usual."

"I wouldn't talk. You're the same way with *Shameless*," I bristled. "So, don't *even*."

"Bitch, *please*. This isn't about me. It's about you," he said with a smirk. "I'm worried about your ass. You seriously need to get out more. If you're not careful, you'll end up being like Old Cat Lady, Mrs. Jergens."

Kai and I were currently renting a house from her, one that used to be her sister's. After the woman died, Mrs. Jergens had decided to rent out the place and the two of us had been living there for the last two years. The woman owned about six cats, if not more, and constantly smelled like ammonia. It was horrible.

"I'm a dog person. It's not going to happen," I replied, as my Chihuahua, Georgie, started barking at me.

"Looks like he knows you're going out and not too happy about it," Kai said, slipping his jacket on.

I picked up Georgie and scratched the top of his head. He was definitely an insecure dog. I'd gotten him from an animal shelter the year before, when he'd been a frightened little puppy. I wasn't sure what had happened to him,

11

but Georgie didn't like many people. He barely tolerated Kai. But, he loved me and hardly left my side when I was home.

"He'll be okay," I said, nuzzling him as I watched Kai check out his reflection in the mirror by the doorway. "Going out?"

He reached over and grabbed his car keys from the console. "Yeah. I'm going to a basketball game."

"Who's dragging you to that?" I asked, knowing he hated every sport but tennis, and only because he played it.

It took him a few seconds to reply. "Trey."

My eyes widened in shock. "What? After everything that happened between you?"

Kai had recently learned that Trey was married to a woman, who apparently had no idea that her husband was bisexual, let alone cheating. Finding out that his boyfriend had an entirely separate life had left him shattered and heartbroken. For weeks, he'd been down-in-the-dumps about it. I couldn't believe he was taking him back.

Kai shoved his hands into his pockets and took a few seconds before answering, almost like he was afraid to tell me. Probably because he knew how I'd react. "He's leaving his wife. He actually told her about us on Christmas."

"Really?" I said dryly.

I disliked Trey even more now, especially because he dropped the bomb on his wife during the holidays. Not only that, I didn't trust him or even feel comfortable around the guy. When he'd stopped over one night looking for Kai, he actually admitted that he'd had a dream about having a threesome with me and Kai. Then, if that wasn't awkward enough, he hinted that he found me fascinating and beautiful. I'd told Kai about it, who'd laughed it off, claiming that Trey was a harmless flirt and had been only trying to warm up to me. I didn't buy that for a minute. The guy was an over-sexed prick who didn't deserve his wife, let alone Kai.

"Yeah, really."

"So, Trey moved out?"

"No. He's going to, though," Kai replied. "I'm glad we're talking about this because he might need a place to stay for few days until he can figure things out."

My jaw dropped. The thought of him staying here made my stomach churn. "*Here?*"

"I know it's an inconvenience, but he has no other place to go."

"What about a motel?" I asked a little harshly, but couldn't help it. It wasn't my fault the guy was in the position he was in.

"He's not working right now. But, he has a job lined up."

12

Trey sold medical supplies, which is how he'd met Kai, who was a pharmacist. "What happened to his other job?"

"I don't know. Some disagreement between him and his boss. Anyway, he just needs a temporary place to crash. Obviously, he'll stay in my room with me. You'll hardly ever see him. Especially, with your hours."

I hated the idea, but Kai was my dearest friend and had been since we'd met in college. I wanted him to be happy and he'd been there for me when I'd needed him. I definitely owed him. I didn't like Trey, but was willing to put up with him for a little while if that's what Kai wanted.

"Fine, but just a few days. This place isn't big enough for three people," I replied.

The house was a two-bedroom rambler with an unfinished basement, built in the eighties. Thankfully, there were two bathrooms, one in my room and one next to the living room, which Kai had claimed. Other than that, there wasn't a lot of privacy or room to move. This never bothered me or Kai, because we clicked so well. But, adding another to the mix, especially someone I didn't care for, was going to suck heavily.

"You're the best," Kai said, giving me a hug. "I'll let him know you're down with it."

More like resigned, I thought. I just hoped that the 'few' days wouldn't turn into anything more permanent, otherwise… best friends or not, my ass was out of there.

"YOU LOOK GREAT," Jessica said when she picked me up, ten minutes later. "I've never seen you with your hair down. It's pretty."

"Thanks," I replied, touching it absently.

"I suppose I should probably warn you, my husband's club brothers are great guys but, they can be a little abrasive."

"Wait a second, when you say 'club'… you mean like the Lion's Club, right?" I asked, thinking back to our earlier conversation.

Jessica laughed. "The Lion's Club? No, honey. Tank is the president of the Gold Vipers. I thought you knew?"

I groaned inwardly. Yes, I'd heard of the Gold Vipers. Hell, everyone in Jensen knew about the notorious biker club. They'd been in the news a few times, although it had been awhile. From what I'd gathered, there'd been a string of murders linked to the club, although there'd never been any convictions.

"No, I didn't."

"This isn't going to be a problem, is it?" she asked, glancing over at me.

I forced a smile to my face. "No. Did you say your stepbrother is the president of the club?"

13

Christmas With The Biker

"Yes, and I know what you're thinking, but there's nothing to be worried about. The guys in the club are not the criminals everyone thinks they are, and they'll be very respectful toward you. Especially because you're with me."

"Okay," I replied, wishing I'd paid more attention to our earlier conversation. I could have feigned other plans or said I had a headache, at the very least. But now it would just be rude to bow out. And cowardly.

"Seriously," she said, after a few seconds of awkward silence between us. "You have nothing to worry about."

"I believe you."

"You know, I totally get your reaction," she said with a little smile. "In fact, I freaked out when I learned my mother had started dating Tank's father. I thought she'd flipped her lid, but Slammer was a good guy and treated her like a queen. I really miss him."

"Slammer?"

"That was his road name. Nickname, you know?"

"Yeah." I noticed she kept saying "was." "What happened to him?"

Jessica's smile faded. "He was murdered."

I was shocked and yet, the news reports were coming back to me. "That's horrible. I'm so sorry for your loss. It must have been a terrible time for your mother and everyone else in his life."

She nodded. "Yeah. It was. My mom still misses the hell out of him."

"I can only imagine. Did they ever find out who did it?"

"Unfortunately, no. They figured it was probably retaliation from another club," she said softly. "Anyway, that was five years ago. Since then, they've made amends with some of their enemies and things have been peaceful."

"That's good," I replied.

"Yeah. Anyway, you'll like the guys. They all look like tough bad-asses, but in reality, they're like big teddy bears. And like I said, as long as they know you're with me, they'll be respectful."

"Okay."

Her face became serious. "Um, but just to be on the safe side, we should probably use the bathroom together—and don't look any of them in the eyes. They really don't like that."

My eyes grew round. "Really?"

Jessica threw her head back and laughed. "Relax. I'm only kidding."

Relaxing, I shook my head and smiled. "That was cruel."

"Sorry. Couldn't help myself."

Amused, I stared out the window as we headed toward the clubhouse. Although she was teasing, I'd heard about biker clubs and how many of the guys had caveman mentalities. I decided that after one or two drinks, I'd feign a headache and call a cab if needed.

14

THREE

GRAHAM

KNOWING IT WAS a party, I asked Jordan to swing by my apartment so I could shower and change. Fortunately, Bonnie wasn't there and neither were her things.

"You live alone?" he asked, when we were inside.

"I do now," I said, the memories of the other day hitting me again like a sledgehammer. "I'm going to take a shower. Make yourself at home."

"Okay. Take your time."

I walked into the bedroom, and the first thing I noticed was the bed. Growling in the back of my throat, I ripped off the sheets and blankets and tossed everything in the corner. I still couldn't believe the fucking bitch had the audacity to not only cheat on me, but do it in my bed. High or not, that was beyond disrespectful. Even the sofa would have been better.

Deciding I'd buy all new linens the following day, I grabbed a change of clothing and took a shower.

I WASN'T SURE what to expect when we pulled up to the gate leading to the Gold Vipers' clubhouse. It was located in the warehouse district and in a building that looked more abandoned than anything, especially with the boarded-up windows. If it hadn't been for the parking lot full of cars and trucks, I'd have never guessed anything was going on.

"That was Zeke," Jordan said, waving to the red-haired guy opening the gate for us. "He's one of the new Prospects. Nice guy. You'll meet him soon, I'm sure."

"What's a Prospect?"

"Someone the club is considering to patch and make a member."

"Makes sense," I replied as we drove forward. "Damn, there are a lot of people here."

"Yeah. Well, this party isn't the norm. The Old Ladies have been invited along other family members. They all want to meet you."

"Great," I mumbled. "No pressure there, right?"

He smiled and pulled around the building where there were more parking spots. Shutting off the engine, he looked over at me. "You okay? You look like you're ready to puke."

I felt like it, too. Knowing everyone was waiting for me reminded me of grade school, when I'd been called up to the front of the room to give a speech. I hated being the center of attention.

"You'll be fine," Jordan said, patting me on the shoulder before getting out of the SUV.

Sighing, I got out too. We walked through the snow, and up the steps, where he knocked on the door. A few seconds later, it opened and another Prospect let us in.

"This him?" the guy asked Jordan.

"Yup. Graham, this is Dover," Jordan said to me.

I held out my hand. "Nice to meet you."

Smiling, he shook it. "You, too. Have fun tonight."

"I will. Thanks," I replied.

Jordan led me down the hallway and to the main part of the clubhouse, which was set up like a bar. Rock music played from a flashy jukebox in the corner, several people wearing Gold Vipers vests were playing pool, and there was wall-to-wall people. It was a big turnout.

"This way," Jordan said, walking away.

I followed him to the bar where several more Gold Vipers appeared to be standing around, shooting the shit.

The tallest of the group noticed Jordan first. A massive guy with short, cropped, dark hair and a neck the size of Texas. Built like a brick shithouse, he looked like he worked out twenty-four-seven. He held his beefy hand out to Jordan. "Hey, brother. I didn't think you were going to actually stop in."

"I figured I'd better walk him inside. He's under enough pressure as it is," Jordan replied, shaking his hand.

"Yeah, I suppose." He turned to me and grinned. "So... *you* must be Graham," he said, holding out his hand. "The name is Tank. Nice to meet you."

I shook his hand. "You, too. We met before, though. At Sal's."

He studied my face and nodded. "Yeah. I guess you do look familiar. I've met a lot of people, but I never forget a face." Tank nodded toward the others standing around the bar, listening quietly. "Let me introduce you to these meatheads. That's Hoss, Cole, Tail, and Chopper."

"Hi. Nice to meet you guys," I replied.

"You, too. So, you just got out of the slammer?" Hoss asked me.

Before I could answer, Tank sighed and scolded the older man. "Jesus, he just walked in and already you're getting personal. You know he did. Why do you think we're having this fundraising benefit?"

"What they get you for?" Hoss asked, ignoring Tank.

"You don't have to answer that," Tank muttered. "Hoss. Mind your own fucking business."

"Hey, I threw a fifty into the pot to bail him out. I think it is my business," he snapped.

"It's okay. Aggravated assault," I said. "Thanks for chipping in."

"No problem. So, he deserve it?" Hoss asked.

"And more," I replied.

Hoss grinned. "Good for you."

"Where's Raptor?" Jordan asked, looking around.

"On his way with Adriana. They dropped the kids off at Frannie's," Tank replied.

"She must have her hands full. She's watching Carissa and Drew, too," Jordan replied.

I'd learned on the ride over that Carissa and Drew were his kids, which would make them my niece and nephew, if what he'd said was true. It was an odd concept to think that not only did I have two brothers, but that I was an uncle.

"Frannie's sister is visiting, so she has help," Tank replied, putting his hand on my shoulder. "In the meantime, I'd better introduce you to the rest of the club."

"You sure you want to do that?" I asked, my stomach tightening.

"What do you mean?" he asked.

"We don't know for sure if I'm related to him or Raptor," I replied. "Shouldn't we wait for a DNA test?"

Tank snorted. "I don't need no fucking DNA test. You look a lot like both of your brothers, especially Raptor. I should know, we grew up together and I can see him in your facial features. So, no. We're not going to wait. Besides, this is a fundraiser. Everyone wants to see you."

"A fundraiser?" I asked.

"Yeah. To recoup your bail. Since we used our annual charity money to get you out of the slammer, we need to raise more for the donation made to the local women's shelter." Tank looked over at Jordan. "I gave Jessica a check before Christmas, by the way. Took it out of the club's slush fund. We'll just replace it with what we bring in tonight."

Jordan nodded. "Yeah, she dropped it off. She said they were thrilled and will be sending you something in the mail here soon."

"I received an email already, too. Speaking of Jessica, here she comes," Tank said, looking past me.

We all turned to see two young women walking toward us. The first one had dark blonde hair and a smile on her face. The second one had lighter hair and large green eyes.

Hoss whistled under his breath. "Damn. Jessica's friend reminds me of that actress in Mama Mia."

"The play?" Jordan asked.

"No. The movie, with Meryl Streep. She looks like the daughter. Amanda something," he replied.

Tank laughed. "Never picked you for a musical lover, Hoss."

"It's the only one I like. Besides Grease," he said. "Anyway, it's not like I watch them all the time or anything."

"Watch what?" Jessica said as the two women stopped next to us.

"Nothing," Hoss replied, giving Tank a warning glare. "Anyway," he smiled at the other woman, "who's your friend, Jessica?"

"Chloe," she replied.

"Hi," said Chloe shyly, smiling at all of us.

We all greeted her.

Looking at me, Jessica smiled warmly and held out her hand. "And you must be Graham. It's so nice to meet you."

I shook it. "You, too. Thanks."

"I was just going to introduce him to the rest of the club," Tank said after drinking the last gulp of his beer. He set the bottle down on the bar and wiped the corner of his mouth. "Come on, brother. Time for you to meet the family."

I followed him through the crowd to a small stage, which I noticed also had a stripper pole. We climbed the steps and he whistled loudly, getting everyone's attention. There had to be close to seventy people in the room.

"Tank!" hollered a few guys, holding their beers up.

He acknowledged them with a nod and a smile and then began to speak. "A couple things… first I'd like to thank everyone for showing up tonight and supporting the fundraiser. Whether you're a member of the club or a close personal friend, it warms me to see so many of you here tonight."

"It could be the tequila that's making you warm, too!" razzed Hoss, laughing at his own joke.

"Yeah, a little of that, too." Tank smirked and scratched the side of his neck. "Anyway, where was I? Oh, yeah… as far as I'm concerned, we're all just one big family and it makes me proud to see us all coming together to look out for each other as well as our community. I just want to add that last week we were able to donate ten-thousand dollars to the local women's shelter. Most of them have young children and you can imagine how crappy it feels to want to make their holidays special but can't afford to. Anyway, with the club's donation, they were able to put some presents under the tree and have a warm holiday meal, so thank you."

The crowd clapped and cheered.

"Where's the money going that's being raised tonight?" asked an older lady with tattoos and biceps bigger than some guys' I'd seen. She was obviously a bodybuilder.

"It's replenishing our slush fund. I wanted to have the fundraiser before the holidays, but we were all so busy. Hopefully next year we'll be more organized and… maybe we can even get Hoss to dress up as Santa Claus," Tank said, glancing toward Hoss.

"When reindeer shit candy canes," Hoss said dryly. "Sorry, brother. But, nobody's sitting on my lap unless she's legal, hot, and willing to unwrap my yule log."

Some people laughed.

"Thanks for that enticing image, Hoss. I think I really *could* use another shot of tequila," Tank replied, chuckling. He turned and put a hand on my shoulder. "Before I do, I want to introduce everyone to Graham Dodge. Thanks to you, we were able to bail him out of jail. If you haven't already heard, he's Raptor and Jordan's long-lost brother."

Everyone raised their drinks and clapped, which was a good feeling. When it quieted down, I also thanked them personally.

"Any brother of Raptor or Jordan is also a brother to us," Tail hollered, raising his beer.

"Thanks. I appreciate it," I replied, still feeling really weird about the idea of having two brothers. I guess at that point, it still felt surreal.

"Are you going to patch him?" one of the women hollered out.

Tank shrugged. "I don't know. Just like everyone else, he'd have to start out as a Prospect and then we'd see if he has the balls to be a Gold Viper."

One of the other women in the group smiled and winked at me. "I wouldn't mind checking that out myself."

Admittedly, she wasn't bad looking and part of me wanted to fuck away every memory I had of Bonnie. But the head on my shoulders was a little too clear at the moment to consider it.

"Now, Candace… that's something you'll have to discuss with him on your own," Tank said as everyone laughed. "Anyway, folks, enjoy the rest of the night and thanks again."

We left the stage, and as we headed toward the bar, a bunch of club members greeted me. I had to admit, the Gold Vipers were much friendlier than I'd imagined them to be.

"You looked a little nervous up there," Jessica teased.

"I was. Tank was talking about raising money and I was standing next to a stripper pole. I thought maybe he was going to make me work for it," I replied.

Everyone laughed.

"Candace would have loved that," Hoss said, grinning. "Although, she's usually the one on the pole."

"That's true. At least from what I hear," said Jessica. "Anyway, Chloe, would you like play some darts?"

"Sure," she replied.

"Jordan?" Jessica said, looking at her husband.

"You sure you want me to play?" he replied with a smirk. "You know I always win."

"You haven't seen Chloe's steady hand. In fact, I might even wager that she'll beat both of us," Jessica said.

Chloe's face turned red and she smiled. "Wait a second… throwing darts and drawing blood are two totally different things."

"Maybe, but it takes a good eye to be successful at both. Have you played darts before?" Jordan asked.

"Only a couple of times," she admitted. "It's been awhile though. I've forgotten most of the games."

"We usually just play 301," said Jessica.

"Okay," she replied.

"Let me know when Raptor gets here," Jordan said, taking off his black leather jacket. "I need to speak to him."

"Will do," Tank replied.

FOUR

CHLOE

THERE SEEMED TO be a lot of eyes on us as we headed over to the two dart machines. Although everyone seemed nice and friendly, there was an undercurrent of arrogance in the room, especially from the fellows wearing the Gold Viper patches. As for the women, there was quite an unusual mix in the crowd. Some looked like tough biker chicks, while others reminded me of the high-maintenance types you'd see on "Real Housewives." The kind with long nails, perfectly groomed eyebrows, and expensive couture clothing.

"I'll be right back. I need to use the bathroom," Jordan said, taking a sip of beer. He set it down on one of the tall pub tables. "Watch this for me, please."

"Will do," she said.

When he left I smiled at her. "Watch his *beer*?"

"I know. He doesn't trust anyone," she whispered, looking amused.

"Is he worried someone will slip him some Rohypnol?"

"Who knows?" she replied. "Although, Raptor's wife had it happen to her."

"Who's that?"

She explained that Raptor was Jordan's half-brother.

"So, now he has two half-brothers?"

"Apparently," she replied.

"It must have been quite a shock."

"Nothing seems to surprise him. Or me, come to think about it. Not since my mother married into the club."

"I can imagine." I swirled the straw around in my Bloody Mary and took a sip.

"So, how's your drink?" asked Jessica, who'd mixed it up for me while Tank and Graham had been onstage.

"Fantastic, thank you. I'm a little hungry and it's actually filling me up," I replied, taking another sip of the cocktail. She'd added a couple olives and a pickle too, which was hitting the spot.

Her eyes widened. "Oh, crap. That's right. We should probably eat something before we both regret it. Do you want to go over and check out the buffet?" she asked, nodding toward the table full of food on the other side of the room.

"Maybe after we play one game?" I replied. "Since, we're already over here." Besides, there was a table full of Gold Vipers sitting next to the buffet and a couple of them were staring at us.

Noticing, Jessica waved at them and they waved back.

"Do you know everyone here then?" I asked her.

"Pretty much. I've never met Graham before."

"What's his story?" I asked, glancing over at him. He was very attractive, even though I normally didn't go for rough looking guys with tattoos. Not to mention they'd had to bail him out of jail. But, he was cute and very intriguing.

"I don't know much, to be honest. Jordan just found out that his mother left Graham in a church when he was an infant, and that nobody knew about it but Slammer."

"Huh. Do you know why he was in jail?"

"Assault, I believe," she replied.

Well, that was that.

Handsome or not, if he'd assaulted someone, I didn't need to hear any more about the guy.

Jessica gave me a funny smile. "Why are you asking?"

"Just curious."

"He's cute, isn't he?" she said with a knowing smile.

I shrugged. "Yeah."

She handed me a set of darts. "But, you're not interested because of the assault."

"I'm not looking for a guy, *period*. Not right now, at least. And if I was, I'd prefer someone without a temper."

The truth was, I wasn't interested in getting involved with anyone. Not after the ordeal I'd gone through with Brent, my last boyfriend, who'd seemed like the perfect guy when we'd first met. After a couple of months, unfortunately, I learned that he was an emotionally abusive, narcissistic asshole. One who'd tried separating me from my friends and family. Thankfully, it was Kai who'd helped me to recognize what kind of controlling and manipulative man Brent really was. Since then, I'd been skittish about getting back into the dating scene.

She nodded. "I don't blame you."

Jordan returned at that moment and the three of us played a couple rounds of 301. Unfortunately, even with my steady hand, I had a horrible aim. Jordan, on the other hand, beat us by a landslide, just like he'd promised.

"That's it. I'm getting hangry," Jessica said, pouting after he buried us again. "I need food."

I set the darts down. "Yeah, I'm hungry, too"

"I'm going to call Raptor and see what's taking him so long," Jordan said, looking at his watch. "Can you get me some food too, Jessica?"

"Sure, babe," she replied.

Smiling, he gave her a quick kiss on the lips and then went to use the phone.

"Your husband is unusually quiet," I said to her. He'd barely said two words during the games.

"Yeah. I happen to talk too much so we're a perfect match," Jessica replied as we headed over to the food.

"How did you two meet?"

"Through Slammer. I'll tell you about it sometime. It's a long story."

"Okay."

"Wow, yummy," Jessica said, when we approached the buffet. "They picked up Olive Garden."

There were several half-eaten trays of lasagna, Fettuccini Alfredo, spaghetti, and ravioli, along with breadsticks and salad. We loaded up three plates in all and found a nearby table. As we started eating, I noticed Graham staring at me. When our eyes met, he looked away.

FIVE

GRAHAM

I THOUGHT I'D feel like an outsider, but the guys were so easygoing and not what I'd imagined a hardcore biker club to be like. Of course, when I'd first met Tank at Sal's, I remembered him to be pretty easygoing. I guess it shouldn't have surprised me that his closest friends had similar demeanors. The only one who seemed a little distant and out-of-place, was Jordan. He didn't say much, except to his wife, and something told me he really didn't want to be at the clubhouse.

"Candace is still checking you out, brother. I'd get all over that before someone else does tonight."

"I heard she left her old man," Tank said in a low voice. "She's probably looking for a revenge fuck. That's probably why she's really even here."

"He cheat on her?" Hoss asked.

"I don't know the details," Tank said, walking around the bar. "Graham, what's your poison? Beer? Cocktail? A shot of whiskey or tequila?"

"I'll take a beer. Thanks," I replied.

"Give him a shot of tequila. He deserves to get fucked up," Hoss said before taking a drag of his e-cigarette.

"You want one?" Tank asked me. "You can stay at the clubhouse tonight if you get too wasted."

"Sure," I replied. "Why not?"

"Maybe Jessica should give him a ride home. If he doesn't get with Candace, she can drop him off with Chloe," Hoss said, staring across the room at her.

"I don't need to get laid," I said, a little amused by the conversation.

"You committed?" Hoss asked.

"Not anymore," I said gruffly.

"Ah, we've all been there, brother. Just remember," Hoss waved his fingers in the air and spoke in sing-song voice, "never underestimate the healing powers of the magical pussy."

"Oh, here we go," Tail said, chuckling. "Hoss giving advice again. Let's hear it, 'Oh wise one'."

"Damn right I'm *wise*. One thing I've learned over the years, it takes one pussy to get over another one." He looked at me. "See, here is what you need to do. You need to bang your way through this town until you've forgotten all about her."

"She's already forgotten," I lied.

His lips pursed as he scowled at me. "Don't bullshit a bullshitter. If you haven't fucked anyone else besides your ex yet, she still *owns* your dick."

The guys laughed at him.

"You think it's funny, but it's true. Tail, you used to be a real baller. Tell him," Hoss said, waving his arm.

Tail looked at me and shrugged. "I mean, he kind of has a point. You won't forget her… but if she's done you wrong and you want to move on, fucking another chick can't hurt."

"See. I told you I was right," Hoss said. "Just because I don't look as pretty as some of you doesn't mean I don't know what I'm talking about. Hell, I've had to work twice as hard to earn my pussy," Hoss said.

"He's lying," Tank said, smirking. "Girls were always hanging on you because of the club. You never had to worry about getting laid."

Hoss smiled. "Okay. That's true. But, I've been hurt in the past. I got over it. Now you know how I did it."

"I hate to say this, but Hoss might be onto something." Tank slid me two shots of tequila. "I also think that after the last couple of days, you could probably use both of these."

"Oh, yeah," I replied. "Thanks."

He grabbed some lime slices and a salt shaker. He moved them toward me. "No problem. Anyone else want a shot?"

"I'll take one," Tail said.

"I'll have one, too," Cole said. "Terin's picking me up so I'm not driving."

Tank poured a few more shots of tequila and we shot them back together, toasting Hoss and his words of wisdom.

"It's about time someone appreciated my advice," he replied with a smug smile.

"We always appreciate you, Hoss," Cole said, patting him on the back.

I could tell by the look on the old man's face he was touched by the sentiment.

"So, Graham, tell us a little about yourself," Tank said to me. "What do you do?"

I told him that I was a master electrician. He then asked me where I'd gone to school and wanted to know about my adoptive parents.

"Sorry to hear they've passed on," he said after I filled them in. "They sounded like good people."

I nodded. "They really were."

"I can't believe you lived in Jensen this entire time and nobody knew about you," Cole said, who I learned was Tank's brother-in-law.

"Yeah. Small world," I replied, haphazardly peeling the label off my beer.

"Did you know you were adopted?" Tail asked.

I nodded. "Yeah. They told me early on."

"Did you ever think about trying to search for your biological parents?" Hoss asked.

"Yes and no. I loved the people who raised me and figured the ones who gave me up had their reasons. I suppose I would have eventually tried tracking them down."

"Seriously, though, I wonder who your old man is," Hoss said, staring at me. "Maybe it's Raptor's? He looks a lot like him, just different hair color."

"He looks like Jordan, too," Tail said.

"He wouldn't be Acid's son," Tank said.

"Who's Acid?" I asked.

Tank told me that Acid had been Jordan's father and one crazy son-of-a-bitch.

"He used to burn him," Hoss said in a low voice, glancing over toward Jordan. "Poor kid was raised by one of the craziest fuckers alive and put up with a lot of abuse. He doesn't talk about it, or anything else really for that matter, but he's *damn* lucky to be alive."

"It made him who he is today, which is still kind of a mystery to most. I suppose it's hard to trust anyone after that kind of life though," Tank said with a sad expression. "Anyway, he's good to Jessica and the kids. We were kind of worried, considering his old man had been such a psychopath."

Listening to them talk about Jordan was sobering. "What about... our mother?" I asked, the words feeling weird on my tongue.

"She was a drug addict," Tank replied. "I didn't know her very much. My old man did, which is why Mavis confided in him. Apparently, they were second or third cousins, too. Damn, I almost forgot about that." Tank grinned. "I guess that makes us related, too."

"I guess so," I answered, smiling back.

"I miss Slammer," Hoss said in a somber voice. "He was the shit."

"A toast to Slammer," Tank said, raising his beer. We all followed suit and drank the second shot.

"I wish I could have met him," I said, the tequila making me warm. "Hell, I wish I could have met her."

"Mavis had actually become clean before...," Tank stopped and his face darkened. "Sorry, man. I shouldn't talk about it."

"Talk about what?" I asked, not understanding.

"Your birthmother's death," Hoss said. "She was murdered by the fucking Devil's Rangers."

I stared at him in shock. "I didn't know that."

"Now, we don't know for sure," Tank replied. "In fact, we finally have somewhat of a truce now, too. It's wise if you don't start bringing that shit up and causing trouble, Hoss."

"The kid deserves to know," he replied.

"Raptor and Jordan can talk to him about that," Tank replied.

"I suppose. You want any more information, you'd better discuss it with them, Dodger," Hoss said.

"It's Dodge," I replied.

Hoss grinned. "I kind of like Dodger. I might just call you that. You have a road name?""

"No," I replied.

"You even ride?" Hoss asked.

I told him about my Hog. "I'm thinking about getting a sled now," I added, hoping I could get the money back for the ring. The fuck if I was going to marry Bonnie now. If I had to sell the damn thing on eBay, I would.

"Some of us have sleds," Tank said. "Once you get one, we'll have to take you out to Hoss's cabin and go riding."

"Yeah. That would be great," I replied and then explained to him about the ring I'd purchased.

"Wow, what a fucking bitch," Tail said.

"At least you found out now before you married her," Hoss said.

"No shit," I replied. "By the way, I'm going to pay you back for bailing me out of jail."

"Don't worry about it," Tank replied, waving his hand.

"Bullshit. I appreciate what you did, but I can't let you pay for my fuckup," I replied.

"It wasn't a fuckup. The asshole deserved it," Hoss said. "He's lucky he got off as easy as he did. If that would have happened to me, he'd be buried in a cornfield right now. You went easy on the prick."

The others nodded and agreed with him.

"Damn, look at that ass," Hoss said staring at someone. "There you go, Dodger. Something to help you start the healing process."

I glanced over and saw Chloe standing at the buffet. Her jeans fit her in all the right places and she was definitely gorgeous, but too sweet-looking. If I was going to fuck anyone tonight, it would have to be guilt-free, and something told me Chloe wasn't into mindless sex. But damn, the tequila had warmed me up all the way to my dick, and the thought of bending Chloe over the buffet was making my jeans tight.

She caught me staring at her and I looked away. As hot as she was, I knew it wasn't what I needed. Or hell, maybe it was. I really didn't have a fucking clue anymore.

"Could I get another shot?" I asked Tank, thinking I'd let the alcohol take over for a while. There was so much going on inside me. I just wanted to forget everything for a while.

"Of course. Like I said, you can drink up and stay the night, brother." He poured me another.

"Seriously, you should hook up with her before someone else does," Hoss said, still ogling Chloe. "Fresh meat like that doesn't walk into the clubhouse often."

"Hoss…" Tank shook his head and looked at me. "Once he gets his mind on something, he can't let it go."

"I'm just trying to help the kid. You're pouring tequila down his throat, fucking him up. I'll get him fucked. A perfect end to a perfect night, if you ask me."

I chuckled.

"I don't know. She works with Jessica. It's not like she's here to get laid. Hell, for all we know she could have a husband waiting for her at home," Tank said.

"I didn't see a ring on her finger," Hoss said.

"It's probably a bad idea," I replied as Tank slid over the shot of tequila. "Although, a few more of these, though, and I'll forget why it's a bad idea."

"Speaking of bad ideas," mumbled Tank, looking past me.

"Hey," said Candace, stopping next to us. She shook her dark brown bangs out of her face and gave Tank a pouty look. "You have any tequila left for me?"

"Sure, darlin'," he replied, grabbing another shot glass from under the bar.

Smiling, she turned to me. "By the way, let me introduce myself." She held out her hand. "The name is Candace. Some people call me Candi."

I had to admit, she had a nice rack and was definitely a looker, but she also looked too made-up and fake for my tastes. Especially with all of the caked-on makeup. Admittedly, her plum-colored glossy lips were a little intriguing to my dick.

I shook her hand. "Graham."

"Here you go," Tank said, sliding over the shot glass. "I imagine you want a lime and some salt?"

"Nah. I can take anything hard… straight," she replied with a wicked gleam in her eyes. "

The guys around us chuckled.

Candace raised the shot glass. "A toast to Graham. May we see a *lot* more of him."

Nodding, I raised my shot and we tossed them back together.

"Whew," she said, shuddering as she set the empty shot glass down. "Now *that* hit the spot."

"What about your other spot, sweetheart?" Hoss asked with a lecherous grin.

She looked over at me and bit the lower corner of her lip. "Oh, Hossy baby, I'm working on filling that one, too."

31

SIX

CHLOE

"THANKS," JORDAN SAID, sitting down next to Jessica and his plate of food.

"You're welcome. What did Raptor have to say?" she asked.

Jordan picked up a breadstick. "He and Adriana just pulled into the parking lot."

"Cool," she replied. "He must be excited to meet Graham."

"Yeah. Apparently, they already met at Sal's. Not as brothers, though," he said.

"Wow, small world," she replied.

"Yeah."

A few seconds later, Raptor and his wife stepped into the clubhouse and Jordan stood up.

"I'll be back in a few," he said.

"Babe, why don't you finish your food? Tank can introduce them," Jessica replied.

"Like I said before, I need to talk to the both of them."

Her eyes narrowed. "What about?"

"It's private. I'll fill you in later," he replied.

Jessica nodded. "Okay. No problem. Could you send Adriana over?"

"Will do," he replied and then headed toward the bar.

"You're going to love Adriana. She's a sweetie," Jessica said before taking a bite of salad.

I glanced over at Graham again and noticed a woman with long, dark hair was hanging on him. Oddly enough, I felt a twinge of jealousy, which made hardly any sense. Sure, he was handsome and had obviously been checking me out, but there was no way in hell I'd get involved with someone like him.

"Looks like Graham's getting laid tonight," Jessica said dryly, also noticing. "Candace certainly doesn't waste any time."

"Who is she?"

"I think she's a Sweet-butt," Jessica replied, her nose wrinkling. "I know she strips, too."

That made sense. She looked like a porn star, fake boobs and all. "What's a Sweet-butt?"

"Someone who parties with the club and is an easy lay," she replied. "Another reason I'm glad Jordan isn't a member. I mean, I know he'd never cheat on me. I just don't need to have my husband surrounded by women like her."

"Yeah, I wouldn't want it either," I replied, nauseated by the way she was hanging on him.

"Oh, here comes Adriana," Jessica said, smiling. She stood up and threw her arms around her friend as soon as she arrived at the table. Adriana looked a lot like the actress, Eva Longoria. "Hey, girl. How've you been?"

"Busy. Tired," she replied, smiling. "The holidays are always crazy. You know how it is."

"Do I ever. By the way, this is Chloe. We work together at the hospital."

"Nice to meet you," she said and then yawned, which made the both of us yawn as well. She laughed. "I'm sorry. I'm making everyone yawn."

"I think we're both tired from working today anyway, so no big deal," Jessica replied. She patted the chair next to her. "Sit down."

"Let me grab some food first," Adriana said, staring at our plates. "Wow, Olive Garden?"

"Yeah," Jessica replied.

"Tank's favorite place. I should have known. I'll be right back," she replied.

I watched Adriana walk toward the food and then stop at the tableful of guys I'd noticed earlier. She chatted for a few seconds and then went to the buffet.

"So, she's your sister-in-law and her husband is the vice-president of the Gold Vipers?" I said.

Jessica nodded. "Yep."

"She doesn't look like I would have imagined her to," I replied, glancing over at Adriana's husband, who was now talking with Graham. Raptor reminded me of the guy who played Thor, in the Marvel movies. Muscular, blonde, with an engaging smile. Very good looking. In fact, there definitely was some resemblance to Graham in his facial features.

"And how was that?" Jessica asked, smiling.

"I don't know. I guess I imagined her to look like a tough cookie or a real badass, you know?" I replied. I wanted to say like a 'biker bitch' but I didn't know if that was offensive or not.

"Believe me, looks are deceiving," she replied. "I'm sure Raptor would be the first to tell you, too."

From the confident way Adriana walked through the tough biker crowd, smiling and even giving some of the guys shit, I believed it.

SEVEN

GRAHAM

C ANDACE WAS COMING on strong by the time Raptor showed up, even offering to give me a ride after the party. I'd never had a woman try so hard with me before. Although I was now as hard as a rock, I didn't want to fuck her. Maybe it was because her slutty attitude reminded me of Bonnie's. Regardless, there was no way I was sticking my dick inside the chick.

"Excuse me," I said, stepping around her to greet Raptor, who was all smiles. Looking at him, I had to admit that I saw a resemblance between us. One I probably would have never picked up if I hadn't known about Mavis though.

"Hey, little brother," he said, opening up his arms. Before I knew what was happening, he was giving me a hug. "Glad you're here."

"Me, too," I answered, feeling an unexpected burst of happiness. I'd been wondering all along whether or not it was all a big mistake, and that maybe I really wasn't Mavis's long-lost son. But standing face-to-face with Raptor, I couldn't deny there was a striking resemblance.

"I wish I would have known about you earlier," he said, studying my face. "Damn, Mavis. I can't believe that after everything, she still kept you from us."

"She sounds like she had a lot of problems," I said, not knowing what else to say.

"You don't know the half of it," Hoss muttered, sipping on his beer.

"Yeah. Unfortunately, drugs messed her up pretty badly," Raptor said.

"Here, brother," Tank said, handing him a beer. "Got a fresh cold one for you."

"Thanks," he replied. "So, Graham, tell me about the family who raised you. Were they decent people?"

Before I could say anything, Jordan appeared by our side. "Sorry to interrupt, but I need to talk to both of you. Can we use your office, Tank?"

"Yeah, sure," he replied, studying him closely. "Something going on?"

"We'll talk later," Jordan said, eyeing the others.

Understanding, Tank nodded.

Raptor grabbed his beer and we followed Jordan through the clubhouse and into the office. Inside was a desk full of paperwork, a laptop computer that had seen better days, and a nudie calendar, dated a few years earlier.

"I think he needs to change his calendar," I said, chuckling.

"That was his old man's," Raptor said. "He leaves it up as a tribute to him."

Jordan closed the door behind us.

"What's this about?" Raptor asked, sitting down on the edge of Tank's desk. "Is something wrong?"

36

"There might be," Jordan replied, walking over to us. He looked at me. "That dirt-bag you beat the shit out of, I just learned that he was found dead about an hour ago."

My eyes widened in surprise. "Seth?"

He nodded.

I smiled. "Karma finally got him. Good."

"Unfortunately, it's not good because someone's trying to set you up to take the fall for his death. Actually, I should say they're trying to set the Gold Vipers up."

Raptor's eyes narrowed. "What do you mean?"

"I got a call from a friend of mine, who works CSI. Apparently, someone carved a 'G' and a 'V' on his chest."

"You're fucking kidding me," Raptor said, looking pissed.

"No. So, I gotta ask you—was this a 'HIT' ordered by the club?" Jordan asked.

"Hell, no," Raptor said. "If it was, do you think our guys would be stupid enough to leave a calling card like that?"

"I had hoped not. I thought it was an idiotic move," he replied with a grim smile.

"Seth is a drug dealer. Maybe it was a deal gone bad?" I suggested.

"He's a small fry, as far as drug dealers go. I'm pretty sure it's someone trying to frame the club," Jordan replied. "Someone who found out about Graham's relationship with it and decided to use the opportunity to strike back."

"Yeah, and I'm sure everyone on the streets knows about it by now," Raptor replied. "Why haven't the cops showed up here yet?"

"I'm sure they will soon," Jordan replied.

"We need to let Tank know," Raptor said, taking out his phone. He sent him a text.

"On another note, how are things going?" Jordan asked me. "I saw you guys laughing and joking around. You seemed to be fitting in pretty well."

"Yeah. The guys are great. I'm just so sorry this is happening now," I replied.

Raptor looked up from his phone. "It's not your fault. Someone is always trying to fuck the Gold Vipers."

I sighed. "Well, whatever it's worth, I'm grateful for everything you've done for me. Bailing me out of jail. Bringing me here. I just hope it wasn't all for naught."

"What do you mean?" asked Raptor.

I looked at both of them. "I hope we're related. I don't have any other family right now and to find out that you two might be my brothers... that's pretty fucking cool. But the truth is, we don't know for sure. Not without a DNA test."

Raptor waved his hand. "We'll have it done, but I don't need a test. Our mugs are way too similar, brother. If I were to dye my hair black, I bet we'd be spitting images of each other." He stared at me hard. "I guess you look a little like Jordan, too. But you and I have the looks that kill."

Jordan grinned and shook his head.

"How old are you guys?" I asked, wondering.

"I'm thirty-two," Raptor said. "Jordan, you've got to be closing in on forty soon, right?"

"Yeah, don't remind me. June."

"So, you're twenty-seven?" Raptor asked me.

"Yeah," I replied. "November 11th was my birthday."

"Happy belated," Jordan said, looking down at his thin leather gloves. I remembered Hoss talking about the acid and wondered how bad his scars were.

"We have a lot of making up to do, little brother," Raptor said, grinning. "First and foremost, though, you interested in joining the club?"

"The Gold Vipers?" I replied, imagining myself riding with them and wearing their patches. It was a different world, I'd been told. Exciting and dangerous. They were both respected and feared by a lot of people. The idea of joining their club was entertaining. "Honestly, I never thought I'd be in a biker club, but I'm liking what I see out there. Everyone seems cool."

"They are cool. We're like one big, happy family," he replied. "Seriously, I think you'd have a lot of fun, although it does take commitment. You'll be doing a lot of riding and will be required to do shit that's not always fun, especially being a Prospect."

"Illegal?" I asked.

"I'm going to be honest," Raptor said. "There might be times when you're asked to do something that could get you in trouble with the law. I can tell you this, though; you will probably get a DUI before you get arrested for whatever you might be asked to do from us. We take care of our members, and if the risk is too great, you won't be involved. I can personally guarantee that."

I nodded. "Okay."

He reached over and patted me on the shoulder. "I'd like to sponsor you. I'm sure we can get you voted in as a Prospect right away, too."

I grinned. "Sweet."

"What about you?" Raptor asked Jordan. "You change your mind yet?"

Grunting, Jordan shook his head. "It's not my thing. I've told you this several times."

"Marriage and kids weren't either. And now look at you," he grinned. "A gorgeous wife. Two kids. A picket fence. Hell, you even have one of those soccer-mom vans."

"It's a crossover," he grumbled.

Raptor chuckled.

Tank walked into the office and saw the scowl on Jordan's face. "What's going on?"

"He's pouting about his minivan," Raptor goaded.

Tank, who had a toothpick in his mouth, took it out and grinned. "Hey, it's a good front, right, Judge?"

Jordan looked at him but didn't say anything.

"Judge, huh? Is that your road name?" I asked Jordan.

"No, and whatever you do, don't ever call me that," he replied, giving Tank a dirty look.

"Sorry. I thought you'd be telling him," Tank said, sitting down behind the desk.

"Tell me what?" I asked.

"Nothing. Let's just drop the subject," he replied.

"And like he said, don't call him that," Tank said.

"No problem," I replied, wondering what that was all about.

Tank sat back in his chair. "So, why am I back here?"

Raptor told him what we'd learned.

Tank sighed. "Fuck. Can't they just let it rest?" he muttered, running a hand over his face.

"They?" Raptor asked.

"It sounds like the fucking Blood Angels. Remember when they carved something into that guy in Minnesota… what the hell is his name again?" Tank said, tapping his fingers on the desk.

"Stan?" Raptor said.

"Yeah, that dude. They probably think we're responsible for killing their prez and decided to stir some shit up for us," he said.

"Who are the Blood Angels?" I asked.

"A rival club. I thought they'd disbanded, though," Raptor said.

"That doesn't mean some of them don't want revenge," said Tank.

"True," Raptor replied.

"It could also be one of the Devil's Rangers," Jordan said.

Tank pulled out his cell phone. "I'm calling Dom. He might have an answer for us."

"Who's that?" I asked, my head spinning from what I was hearing. Club presidents being assassinated. Rival clubs wanting to frame the Gold Vipers. Did I really want to involve myself?

"Dom is the V.P. of our St. Paul Chapter," Raptor explained. He lowered his voice. "He's also psychic."

I definitely didn't believe in that shit, but from the looks on Tank's and Raptor's faces, they did.

"So, Graham... You still interested in joining the club?" Jordan asked with a smirk.

EIGHT

CHLOE

A S THE NIGHT wore on, the crowd in the clubhouse became pretty rowdy, especially the guys, which wasn't really a surprise. Arm-wrestling broke out, as did drinking games, poker, and even a karaoke contest. Apparently, even bad-assed bikers enjoyed getting drunk and making fools out of themselves in front of a mic once every in a while. It was all in good fun, however, and I actually really enjoyed myself.

"So, Chloe… do you have a boyfriend?" Adriana asked, smiling at me over her drink. The three of us were feeling pretty good, especially after drinking a round of kamikaze shots, which one of the bikers had brought over. A guy named Tail, who was super sweet and not at all bad looking. I'd learned that he used to be a real man-whore until he met Lauren, his wife. With his bedroom eyes and drop-dead good looks, I could see why.

"Not right now," I replied, noticing the way her eyes were sparkling. "Why?"

"See the guy arm-wrestling over by the pool tables," she said, nodding toward two burly-looking men staring at each with red faces. "The one with the short blond hair and goatee? He was asking."

The man she was talking about looked like he was in his late thirties, and had huge arms covered in snake tattoos. I'd noticed him over by the buffet earlier, checking me out. He wasn't bad looking, but loud and a little too obnoxious.

"Oh," I said, returning my gaze to Adriana. "I'm not really looking for one right now."

She laughed. "I don't think he wants to actually fill *that* position."

"I think we all know what he really wants to fill, and probably in many positions," Jessica said in a low voice, smiling wickedly.

We all laughed.

"To be honest, I'm not into one-night stands either." Plus, he was a little scary looking.

"I hear you," she replied.

"Adriana… do you know anything about why Graham was in jail?" Jessica asked.

"All I know is that he beat some guy up he found in his apartment. That's what Trevor told me, at least," she replied.

"Who's Trevor?" I asked.

"My husband," Adriana replied.

"Raptor," clarified Jessica. "They all have these road names. Even the women."

"Ah," I replied. "What about you two?"

Jessica shook her head.

"Trevor calls me Kitten sometimes," Adriana said with a small smile.

Jessica sat back in her chair and stared past me. "Speak of the devils."

Adriana's eyes narrowed. "I wonder what their little pow-wow was about?"

I looked over my shoulder and saw Jordan, Raptor, and Graham walking out of the back room. I couldn't help but notice how sexy Graham looked with his jacket off, especially in his low-riding jeans and simple black T-shirt. My eyes grazed over his muscular biceps, broad shoulders, and lean waist. He obviously had great genes and were shared by the two guys next to him.

"They look so serious," mused Jessica, playing with her straw.

"Yeah and that's what worries me," Adriana replied.

Jordan and Raptor headed toward us, while Graham went back over to the bar. Noticing the way his jeans hugged his ass reminded me of how much I missed having sex. *Needed* to have sex. The toy in my nightstand could only do so much, and there was nothing like wrapping one's legs around a man's waist and feeling every inch of him.

Oh, God. The alcohol was kicking in.

"Hey, babe," Adriana said, as Raptor came up behind her and kissed her on the side of neck. "What's up?"

"Nothing," he replied, raising his head back up. He began massaging her shoulders. "Just getting to know Graham a little better."

"Right," she said dryly and then looked over at me. "By the way, meet Chloe. She works with Jessica at the hospital."

He smiled. "Hey, Chloe. Nice to meet you."

"You, too," I replied, admittedly feeling a little nervous. He was the V.P. of the Gold Vipers, and obviously well respected by many. He was also feared by many, I suspected.

"You almost ready to go?" Jordan asked Jessica.

She looked at me. "I don't know. What do you think?"

"Yeah, whenever you're ready," I replied. I knew drinking any more would be dangerous, and if I wasn't careful, I'd end up making some bad decisions.

Jordan's eyes narrowed. "How much have you had to drink, Jess?"

She shrugged. "A couple cocktails and a shot. I spaced them out, though. I'm fine."

He didn't look like he believed her.

Noticing his expression, Jessica groaned and stood up. "Here, look," she said standing on one foot. She closed her eyes and touched her nose with one hand and then the other.

With an evil smile on his face, Jordan poked her in the shoulder and she stumbled backward on her heels.

Gasping, she stomped back to him, her cheeks pink. "You ass," Jessica pouted, trying to keep a straight face. "I ought to—"

Jordan reached for her, kissing away the rest of her words.

Smiling, I turned and found myself locked in a gaze with Graham again, who'd obviously been watching the exchange. He grinned back at me and I couldn't help but think again how handsome he was.

Maybe I'm being too critical of the guy?

I couldn't exactly blame him for beating up some asshole who'd been trespassing in his home.

"What about Graham?" Raptor asked. "I doubt he'll want to leave right now. Should I give him a ride later?"

"I don't think he's going to need one," Jordan replied. "I think someone else already has that covered."

Sure enough, the woman from earlier was already back at the bar and practically on his lap.

God, what a slut.

I couldn't exactly blame her, however. Turning away, I reminded myself that it was silly for me to feel jealous and blamed it on the alcohol again.

"Leave it to Candace," Raptor said, smirking. "Well, he probably could use some TLC after spending a couple nights in jail."

"You might want to let him know that he should probably get a tetanus shot after a night with her," mused Jessica. She reached into her purse and pulled out her car keys. "You ready to go, Chloe?"

"Yeah. I should probably use the bathroom first," I replied.

"Okay. I'll show you where it is," she replied.

We left the table and I followed her to the restroom, which there was a line of two others waiting to get in. As we stood there, Jessica's phone rang.

"Huh, it's Frannie," she said.

She answered the phone and walked away from the bathroom line. A few seconds later, she came back over, a concerned look on her face. "One of my kids is throwing up, apparently. Drew."

"Oh no," I replied. "I wonder if it's that flu that's going around?"

"Probably. One of his friends had it a couple of days ago," she replied and sighed. "I'd better tell Jordan so he can leave now. I'll meet you back at the table."

"Okay."

She walked away, and soon I was able to use the bathroom. After I was finished, I stepped out of the bathroom, rounded the corner, and walked right into Graham's chest.

"Oh, sorry," I replied, backing up, embarrassed that I'd also stepped on his foot.

44

"No problem. I have another foot. Chloe, right?" he replied, staring down at me, his dark eyes twinkling.

For some reason, I was totally nervous standing there. Almost like a teenager talking to her crush for the first time. Not knowing what else to say, I asked him a dumb question. "Yes. Where's your friend?"

He gave me a puzzled look. "My friend?"

"Ms. Spider Monkey," I replied, wishing I wouldn't have brought her up. "Candace."

Graham laughed. "She's not a friend. In fact, I'm using the bathroom as an escape."

"Good luck with that. Let me get out of your way then."

"You're not in my way," he said, staring at me with the kind of interest that made my stomach whirl.

Noticing Candace heading toward us, I warned him.

Swearing, he grabbed my hand and pulled me around the corner. "I could really use your help."

I stared up at him in confusion. "With what?"

In answer, he pulled me into his arms and began kissing me.

NINE

GRAHAM

Cassie Alexandra

Two minutes earlier...

CANDACE WASN'T GETTING the hint. The chick was all over me and I was sure a lot of guys would be thrilled. Not this guy. Truth was, she was bugging the shit out of me. Unfortunately, Tank was in his office and Jordan and Raptor were busy with their wives at the moment. The other guys were discussing club shit and I wasn't much of a conversationalist anyway, which is how she ended up on my lap, I guess.

"Hey, I overheard your ride is leaving," she said, running a hand over my thigh. "How about I give you a lift home?"

"Thanks, but… I'm not really sure when I'll be leaving. It could be late."

"It's okay, I'm not in a hurry," Candace said, touching my zipper. She smiled wickedly. "Well, maybe a little bit."

"Whoa," I said, grabbing her hand. I needed to get away from her before I ended up doing something I'd regret. "You know, I think I need to use the bathroom."

Candace leaned in to me. "I think it feels like you need something else," she whispered near my ear.

Yeah, maybe. But definitely not by you.

I pushed her gently away and stood up. "I'll be back."

"I'll be waiting. Did I tell you I'm not wearing panties?" she whispered.

Fuck.

I didn't have to use the men's room. What I needed was a few minutes to myself.

I headed toward the bathroom and that's when Chloe rounded the corner, and we collided.

"Oh, sorry," she said, staring up at me with those big emerald eyes. Her cheeks turned pink.

"No problem. I have another foot," I said, smiling at her. "Chloe, right?"

She nodded and looked around. "Yes. Where's your friend?"

I raised my eyebrow. "Which one?"

"Ms. Spider Monkey. Candace."

I laughed "She's not a friend. In fact," I smiled wryly. "I'm using the bathroom as an escape."

"Good luck with that. Let me get out of your way then."

"You're not in my way." Not in the least. The girl was seriously gorgeous. Flawless, peach skin. Cat-eyes. Lips that were full, glossy, and heart-shaped. Plus, she was wearing this soft green sweater that hugged her tits in a way that made my mouth dry.

Chloe's eyes widened as she looked past me. "Uh, oh. Here she comes."

"Fuck." I pulled her around the corner and into the hallway. I knew if I didn't do something quickly, Candace wasn't going to leave me alone, and eventually, we might just end up fucking. If I was going to bang anyone, I didn't want it to be a slut like her. She was obviously one of the club whores, willing to spread her legs for any of the Gold Vipers or their close, personal friends. I decided to take a chance on Chloe and hoped she wouldn't get too offended and slap my face. "I could really use your help," I told her.

She stared up at me, confused. "With what?"

Hearing Candace's footsteps quickly approaching, I pulled Chloe into my arms and began kissing her. At first, she was rigid in my arms, but then to my relief, she began kissing me back.

Seeing us, Candace growled in the back of her throat. "Prick."

Ignoring her, I gave all my attention to Chloe, whose lips were soft and tasted sweet, like berries. Taking it a step further, I slid my tongue into her mouth and pushed her against the wall, forgetting it was supposed to be an act. Hungry and horny as hell, I slid my hand into her hair and held her in place as we kissed, surprised at the chemistry between us and how much I wanted her.

"Ahem."

Recognizing Jessica's voice this time, we separated quickly.

"Wow, I leave you alone for a minute… and this happens," Jessica said with an amused gleam in her eyes. "I can't take you anywhere."

Chloe looked horrified. "It… we were just faking it," she said, her cheeks red.

"Right," Jessica said dryly.

I cleared my throat. "She's right. Candace was heading toward us and Chloe was gracious enough to play along with me. Thanks, by the way."

Avoiding my eyes, she nodded. "Yeah. No problem."

"You're trying to *avoid* Candace?" Jessica asked, looking surprised. "I guess now I know why she looked so pissed off a few seconds ago."

"Yeah. The chick has been all over me. It's irritating," I replied.

"Hmm… Funny, most guys wouldn't have a problem with that," Jessica said, eyeing me suspiciously.

I shrugged. "I'm not—"

"Most guys," Jessica finished, smiling. "Well, bravo. You two sure had me fooled. And her too, from the way she stomped away."

"Good," I replied.

"Anyway, I hate to break up this little escapade, but we have to leave. You ready, Chloe?" Jessica asked.

She nodded.

I suddenly longed to get the fuck out of there, too. As much as I appreciated the party and everything the club had done for me, I was both physically and mentally exhausted. Having spent the last two nights in jail, all I really wanted was to go back to my place and crash.

"Have a good night, Graham," Jessica said. "It was nice meeting you."

"You, too," I replied.

Jessica looked at Chloe. "You sure you don't want to stay? I can probably find you a ride home."

"No. I'm ready," she replied. "Goodbye, Graham."

"See you around," I said, actually hoping we might run into each other again.

She smiled and the two walked away.

TEN

CHLOE

"OKAY, WHAT IN the hell was *really* happening in there?" Jessica asked as we walked out of the club and toward her car. It was so cold, we could see our icy breath in the air. "I mean seriously, you two didn't have to make out in order for him to tell Candace to take a hike."

"I was just as surprised as you were, honestly. I didn't see it coming," I replied, still shaken from the kiss.

We got into her car and she started the engine. "I think he was just using it as an excuse to try and get with you," she said, rubbing her hands together for warmth.

"He didn't kiss me until I told him that Candace was walking toward us," I pointed out.

"Well, maybe he really was trying to piss her off then."

I nodded.

"There are probably a lot of cops out. I'm fine to drive but I should probably do something about my breath." She reached into her purse and grabbed a stick of gum. "You want one?"

"Sure. Thanks."

Jessica handed a piece to me. "So, tell me… was he a good kisser?"

"Oh, my God… yes. He was a *fantastic* kisser," I replied, smiling.

Her eyes twinkled. "You should have stayed. Or at the very least, gotten his number."

Despite the amazing kiss, I still couldn't help but be wary of someone who'd been released from jail a few hours ago. Whether or not the guy he beat up deserved it or not, I wasn't comfortable with having sex with someone with a temper. Been there. Done that. I told her my feelings about dating someone like that.

"Yeah. I guess I can't blame you," she replied, after I told her my thoughts. "There's certainly a lot of other fish in the sea."

"And, like I said, I'm not looking for anything right now."

"Not even casual sex? I suppose there's always Tinder."

I grimaced. "Yuck. That's definitely not my thing. Don't get me wrong… I miss being with a guy." *Boy, did I miss it.* "But, I'm willing to wait until the time is right."

"Good for you. Some women think they can't live without a man in their lives. It's a shame, too. Anyway, I wasn't looking for anything when I met Jordan."

"How did you two meet?"

She smiled. "Like I said before, it's a long story. One of these days I'll have you over. We'll share a bottle of wine and I'll tell you all about it."

"Sounds great. Thanks for everything tonight, by the way. It was nice to get out."

"You're welcome. The next time they throw a family-friendly party like this, I'll see if you want to join me again."

"Family-friendly, huh?"

She laughed. "Yeah. In fact, the Old Ladies aren't usually invited to the crazy parties because they get so nuts. Tank has told me about some of the things that go on, and it gets pretty bad."

"Another reason you're glad Jordan isn't a club member?"

Jessica nodded. "Definitely. I mean, I'm sure Raptor and Tank behave themselves around the club whores and strippers. They love their wives. But, they're still exposed to temptation, which is why I'm glad Jordan prefers to stay out of the club."

"I don't blame you," I replied, imaging what it would be like to be in a relationship with one of the Gold Vipers and knowing there were girls like Ms. Spider Monkey hanging around. It definitely wasn't something I could handle.

We talked the rest of the way home about work and then I told her about my roommate getting back together with his boyfriend.

"Sounds like you're not happy about that."

"No. I don't trust him."

"That's too bad. Hopefully, Kai won't get hurt by him again."

"I hope not. Otherwise maybe I should send the Gold Vipers after him," I joked.

"The very threat would probably scare him straight," she said, laughing.

"I don't care as long as he chooses a side and sticks to it," I replied.

After she brought me home, I stepped into the house and groaned at the sight of Trey's luggage sitting near the entryway. They'd apparently dropped his things off and then went on their date.

And so it begins, I thought glumly, hoping Kai's boyfriend would land a job and get the hell out as soon as possible. Unfortunately, I wasn't so lucky…

ELEVEN

GRAHAM

LESS THAN TWELVE MONTHS LATER

"TANK AND RAPTOR are looking for you," said Ice, AKA Cole, who was brushing a fresh layer of snow from his truck. I'd just pulled up to the clubhouse after finishing some electrical work at Sal's. Raina, Cole's sister and Tank's wife, was remodeling and wanted to turn the place into a family restaurant. Right now it was nothing but a hole-in-the-wall and there was still a shitload of work to be done. Fortunately, my part was finished and I also had the next few days off of work. A couple guys in the club had invited me to go snowmobiling over the weekend, and I was looking forward to relaxing and having fun.

"Yeah, Raptor sent me a message. Where you off to?"

"Christmas shopping," he replied. "For Terin. Last year I waited until the last minute to buy her something and I'm not making that mistake again."

"I don't blame you. The weekend is going to be horrible with last-minute shoppers."

"You doing any shopping?"

"Fuck no," I replied, smiling. "I hate crowds, especially during the holidays. I ordered all my shit online." This year my list was much longer than usual. My family tree had grown substantially, and it now it even included nieces and nephews.

"At least you don't have a chick to buy for," he replied, opening up the back door and tossing the snowbrush inside. "I gave Terin a new vacuum last year for Christmas. You know… one of those Roombas that do the job for you? I thought it was as cool as shit, especially since she was always complaining about not having enough time to vacuum. You should have seen the look on her face when she opened it. I thought she was going to reach for her gun."

I laughed. Terin, his wife, was a cop. "Dude, you don't give your woman something like that for Christmas. Unless you're going to follow it up with a pair of earrings or something sentimental."

He grinned sheepishly. "Yeah, I should have known better. Another reason why I'm doing my shopping tonight. I'm thinking about getting her this ring she was eyeing at Adriana's store. That's where I'm heading now."

Remembering the engagement ring I'd purchased for Bonnie the year before took the smile from my face. Fortunately, I'd been able to return it and buy my sled, but the memory of what had happened still stung like a son-of-a-bitch.

"Have fun," I said, turning around and walking toward the doorway, shoving Bonnie's memory out of my thoughts. I was done with commitments and, hell, women in general. Sure, I partied with them and had an occasional one-night stand. But frankly, I trusted a woman as much as a preacher who lived in Beverly Hills and drove a Beemer. Most of my time and respect went toward the club and my brothers. They were now my world and I was finally beginning to feel like I really fit in.

"Thanks. See you later."

I waved at him over my shoulder and continued on my way.

"There he is," Tank said when I walked inside the clubhouse. "The man of the hour."

I stomped the snow off of my boots and smirked. "Oh, shit. What do you need me to do now?"

I'd been a Prospect for the last ten months and they were always giving me shit to do that nobody else wanted. I didn't mind, though. I'd become really close with everyone the last year, especially Raptor and Tank. Jordan was cool, too, but never around, and when he was, he hardly said anything. It was just his way and I was getting used to it.

Tank laughed. "Brother," he said, putting his hand over his heart. "Can't I just give you a warm welcome? Especially on this cold-assed blustery day?"

"You could, but then I'd have to drive you to the E.R. to find out what kind of head trauma you received and if they can fix it," I said wryly.

"That's *definitely* your brother," he replied, smiling at Raptor.

"And he's got your number," Raptor replied.

"Mine? You're the one who volunteered him."

I looked at Raptor. "For what?"

He shifted in his chair and then smiled. "How do you feel about kids?"

I frowned. "I like yours." I nodded toward Tank. "His, too. Jordan's are pretty cool as well. Other than that, kids are great as long as they're not in my way. Why?"

Tank started laughing and Raptor gave him a warning look.

"Okay. What the hell is going on?" I asked, smiling.

"Being a Prospect means you have to commit yourself to tasks that you don't always find... enjoyable," Raptor said.

I walked over to where they were sitting, at one of the pub tables. "Yeah. I've figured that out. Especially last week when Tank asked me to help clean out the grease trap at Sal's."

"Oh, shit. That's right. I'd forgotten about that," Tank replied looking amused.

"Thanks, by the way. I don't think that thing was ever cleaned," I replied, remembering the smell and the mess.

55

"Raina was really grateful for all your help," he replied. "She says you're doing an awesome job with the electrical stuff, too."

"I'm glad she's pleased," I said truthfully. "Now, spill it. What did you sign me up for?"

"How are your 'ho, ho, hos?" Raptor asked with a mischievous grin.

TWELVE

CHLOE

"I STILL FEEL like shit about this," Kai said, as we set down the last of the moving boxes into my new apartment. "I wish you weren't moving out. I know you're upset about Trey, but he really does like you and feels just as bad as I do."

I bit my tongue, knowing that whatever I said wouldn't make a difference. Kai was still madly in love with Trey, who was as manipulative as ever. Unfortunately, he was also blinded by that love and unwilling to see the man for who he really was—a selfish and lazy prick. During the last year he'd basically wormed his way into our lives and hadn't contributed anything toward rent or housing expenses. Yes, he was working part-time, but his money went toward who knows what. Kai kept making lame excuses for him and I'd stopped asking questions long ago.

"This is for the best," I replied, staring at the walls of my new place, relieved I wouldn't have to live with Trey any longer. Just seeing the man made me so damn angry. Fortunately, he'd kept his paws to himself and had only flirted a couple of times. Realizing I wasn't interested, and in fact annoyed as hell, he'd given up and we'd ignored each other for the most part. There was one time, however, when he'd walked in on me in the bathroom. I'd been taking a shower and had apparently forgotten to lock the door. Of course, I'd also thought I was the only one home. I'd screamed and Trey had claimed he hadn't heard the water running, which was bullshit. I knew better. Fortunately, he hadn't seen much of me, only a blur through the frosted glass, but I still felt violated by the incident.

"Are you sure you don't want any help unpacking?"

"No, but thank you. I need to run to the store and pick up a few items before I start anyway. I'll probably leave here right after you do."

"Okay. By the way, Renee said you can visit Georgie whenever you want," he said.

My heart felt heavy just thinking about Georgie. I couldn't have him in the apartment, as they didn't allow pets. I'd struggled with letting him go, but in the end found a solution that was bittersweet. Kai's niece, Katie, had been wishing for a dog for Christmas, but they couldn't afford one. It was my gift to her. I knew Katie would take very good care of Georgie, who had grown attached to her quickly.

"Thank you," I replied, trying not to cry as a wave of emotions rushed through me. I was losing both Kai and Georgie. Sure, I could still see them, but it would never be the same.

He nodded and then gave me a hug. "If you ever need anything, call me. I don't care if it's in the middle of the night," he said softly.

"Thanks. Same goes for you."

Kai released me and I walked him to the door.

"Kai."

He turned and looked at me.

"You only live once, so be good to yourself," I said, remembering our old saying we used back in college. It had been more of a joke and we'd used it on everything, whether it was choosing something on a menu or buying an expensive article of clothing. I just wish he'd remember the motto when it came to relationships.

His eyes softened. "You, too."

We said our goodbyes and then he took off. I could tell he felt guilty, but his love for Trey outshined everything. Sadly, that included our friendship.

An hour later, I was battling the crowds at the store. I should have known better, since it was the holiday season. But I wanted my own Christmas tree and was determined to get one up before I went to bed that night. Call it silly, but I really needed some festiveness in my life, especially after moving away from my best friend. As I was contemplating which tree to buy, my cell phone rang. It was Jessica.

"Hi, how's the move going?" she asked in a cheery mood.

"It's been a lot of work, but I just got the last of the boxes into my apartment," I replied, walking by a frosted pine tree.

"Would you like some help unpacking? I just finished my shift."

"No. But thank you for the offer." I knew she'd be tired anyway, and I had the next couple days off to unpack.

"Are you sure?"

"Yes. I'm actually at the store purchasing a Christmas tree."

"You are? Oh, that reminds me… the Gold Vipers are going to be holding another fundraiser this year and are looking for volunteers to help out. They're trying to raise money for the homeless *and* the Children's Cancer Research Organization."

"Cool."

"They're also sending Santa Claus over to the hospital on Friday to pass out presents to the children. They need an elf to help him out, preferably someone who knows their way around. I'm working, otherwise I'd do it."

"I can do it, if they haven't found anyone else yet."

"I don't think they have."

"What time?"

"Around eleven."

"That time works for me. I'm not back at the hospital until Sunday night, and I can't wait to see the looks on the children's faces when they see Santa," I replied, smiling.

"You're a doll. Thank you. I'll let Tank know. Should I have him call you?"

"Yeah. I'm also free on Friday if they need any other help."

"Actually, Tank might take you up on it. They've rented out some banquet room downtown for children to meet Santa. They're going to charge for pictures and donate all the proceeds. They need volunteers for that, too."

"I'm available. Let him know."

"You sure you won't be too busy?"

"I'm never too busy for holiday fundraisers."

"I'll tell Tank. He was hoping you'd be available."

Me specifically?

"Really?"

"Well, I told him that you mentioned something about being able to help out this holiday season. He must have remembered. Of course, not a lot of bikers want to dress as elves. So, that's probably why he was hoping *you'd* volunteer."

I chuckled. "Makes sense."

We'd talked about it last year, after the party at the clubhouse. I'd been a little tipsy on the ride home, volunteering my time freely without thinking. But, I loved Christmas and needed something to cheer me up. This sounded like fun and it was for a great cause. Plus, I'd heard Graham was now a Prospect and secretly hoped to run into him. I still wasn't crazy about the jail thing, but I wasn't planning on marrying the guy. Not even date him. I just wanted to see him again. I'd spent many nights thinking about him; hell, *fantasizing* about him. I just wanted to see if he was as sexy as I'd remembered. Bad boys weren't my thing in the real world, but, fantasies were different. They were safe, no matter who I chose to be my partner.

"Anyway, I'm going to call him and let him know you're in."

"Sounds good."

We spoke for a few more seconds and then hung up. A short time later, I had a new tree in my cart and was racking up over three hundred dollars for lights and decorations, but didn't care. I was determined to make it beautiful. After all, a person only lives once...

THIRTEEN

GRAHAM

AFTER MY TALK with Raptor and Tank, I was grumpier than shit. They'd basically put a kibosh on my relaxing, fun-filled weekend. Instead of snowmobiling, I would spend the next few days wearing a red suit and a white beard. If that wasn't bad enough, I'd have to pretend to be jolly for the kids, which was going to drive me to drink. I had a feeling as to why Santa's eyes were always twinkling. He was half-in-the-bag most of the time.

I knew dressing up and playing him was for a good cause and everything, but I was not the right guy for the job. Hell, I wasn't even looking forward to Christmas. I hadn't even put up a goddamn tree, wanting the season to be over as quickly as possible. Unfortunately, there wasn't anything I could do about it unless I wanted to turn in my Prospect cut, disappointing both my brother and Tank.

Fuck.

I walked out of the clubhouse, needing some fresh air. The snow was coming down harder and I saw Cleaner in the parking lot, trying to plow around the vehicles with a small tractor. He saw me and waved me over.

"What's up?" I asked.

He handed me a bunch of keys. "Can you help me move some of these vehicles so I can get some of this snow out of the parking lot?" he asked loudly.

"Sure," I replied, taking them from him.

"Thanks." He reached into his pocket and pulled out a pack of smokes. "It would have been nice if the guys would have just volunteered to move their own vehicles. But, they like to see me running."

"You and me both. It's payback."

"Yeah." He lit his cigarette.

I stared at the snow coming down. "Why don't you just wait until this shit stops?"

"It's not going to. We're going to get dumped on for the next several days," he replied. "And most of us are heading out this weekend to go snowmobiling. I want to make sure Tank and the other guys can get in and out of the parking lot."

My eye twitched. "Okay."

Cleaner blew out a cloud of smoke and smiled. "I heard you're going to be playing Santa Claus. I thought for sure they were going to make *me* do it."

He was also a Prospect, and although he was younger than me, he looked more the part. A burly guy with a slight paunch, dimples, and bright blue eyes. He always had a smile on his face, even when he was picking up after everyone, which was often. He had O.C.D. and couldn't leave a room without cleaning something up first. Truth was, I'd never seen the clubhouse look so spotless until he'd arrived.

"Nope. Guess, I'm the lucky bastard," I muttered.

"Come on, man. It won't be so bad. You look like someone just pissed in your Wheaties," he replied, looking amused.

"You want to switch with me?"

He laughed. "Fuck no. Like I said before… I've got the weekend off and I'm going to put some miles on my sled."

"Yeah. Lucky you," I said dryly. "I thought I did, too." My sled had very little miles on it. I'd purchased it in October and it was being stored at Hoss's cabin, since I lived in an apartment.

"Did you tell them you had other plans?" he asked, studying me.

I shook my head. I hadn't, which was my own fault. But, somehow I thought they'd already known anyway. "I doubt it would have made a difference."

"Probably not, but you should have said something. Raptor's your brother. He might have let you off the hook."

"I don't need any special treatment."

I knew some of the other Prospects thought I'd get off easier because of Raptor, but it seemed like just the opposite. Which was why I hadn't complained when I'd heard the news about playing Santa Claus. As mad as I'd been, I'd kept my mouth shut and hadn't said a word about how pissed I'd really been.

He stared at me for a few seconds more and then nodded toward the vehicles. "Let's get those cages moved so we can finish this shit up. Afterward, if they let us go, I'll buy you a beer."

"Sounds good," I replied.

AN HOUR LATER, we'd managed to clear out most of the parking lot. Thankfully, the snow had tapered off and wasn't supposed to pick up again for a few hours.

After putting the tractor away, we walked back into the clubhouse and handed keys back to the remaining club members who were still there.

"Anything else you need done?" Cleaner asked when we approached Tank, who'd just gotten off the phone with someone.

"You can go home, Cleaner," he replied and then looked at me. "You can, too. *After* you drop something off for me first. It looks like it should be on your way anyway."

"Sure," I said, relieved. "Where to?"

He tore off a piece of paper he'd written something on and handed it to me. "Here's the address. I need you to drop off the package that's sitting on my desk to that place."

I looked down at the address. "Is this an apartment complex or a business?"

"Apartment."

I nodded. "I'll go and grab the package then. Anything else?"

He grinned. "Nope."

Tank look amused and I wondered if something was up. Before I could ask any more questions, his phone rang again. He answered it. "You see that look on his face?" Cleaner said as we walked away.

"I noticed."

"Wonder what that was about?"

"Maybe he's imagining me in a Santa suit," I said dryly.

He chuckled. "I have to admit, that is kind of a funny vision. You as a jolly old elf. If I wasn't going snowmobiling this weekend, I'd take pictures and heckle you all weekend."

I flipped him off.

FOURTEEN

CHLOE

THE ROADS WERE starting to get very slippery and everyone was driving slowly. Almost *too* slowly. By the time I made it home, I was too tired to do much of anything, so I decided to unpack some of my clothing and then get to the Christmas tree. As I was deciding where to put it, my cell phone rang. It was a phone number I didn't recognize.

"Hello?"

"Hey, is this Chloe Wilson?"

I groaned inwardly. The guy sounded too cheery to be anything but a telemarketer. "Yes."

"It's Tank. I don't know if you remember me, but we met last year at the Gold Vipers' fundraiser."

"Of course, I remember you," I said, relaxing. "How've you been?"

We chatted for a while about the last few months and then he brought up the fundraiser.

"Tomorrow we could use a few people to hand out invites for our 'Meet Santa' fundraiser. I was just wondering if you'd have an hour or two to help pass out some flyers?"

That sounded easy enough. "Sure. I would love to," I replied.

"Awesome. There's one more thing. You need to dress like an elf. I have a costume for you, so don't worry about finding anything to wear."

It sounded like fun and I loved dressing up. After Christmas, my favorite holiday was Halloween. "No problem. As long as it's not too revealing and my ass isn't hanging out."

He chuckled. "No. Not at all. It's family-friendly, although you've given me some ideas for next year. At least for my wife, Raina."

I smiled. "Oh, boy. Well, I'm glad I could help. Um, so… do you want me to stop by the clubhouse to pick up the costume?"

"No. I hear the roads are getting bad. Why don't you give me your address and I'll have someone drop it off?"

Relieved I didn't have to go back out onto the icy roads, I gave him the information.

"Great. Thanks again. We really appreciate you wanting to help out."

"It's for a good cause. I don't mind at all."

"I wish everyone had your attitude," he said, sounding a little exasperated. "Anyway, try on the elf costume. It should fit, but if it doesn't, let me know."

"Will do. When do you think someone will be dropping it off?"

"Hopefully, within the hour."

"Okay. I'll watch for them."

FORTY-FIVE MINUTES LATER, my intercom buzzed. I stepped away from the Christmas tree, which I'd just finished stringing lights onto, and answered it.

"Hello?"

"I have a package for you from Tank," the man said briskly.

"Okay."

I buzzed the stranger in, and a few seconds later, there was a sharp rap on the door. I opened it up and when I saw who was standing in the hallway, my stomach did a flip-flop. It didn't help that he looked even more handsome than I'd remembered. "Oh. Hi."

Staring at me in surprise, Graham seemed just as shocked to see me. "Hi."

Unable to get the stupid smile off my face, I looked at the package he was holding. It was wrapped in brown paper and had my address scribbled on the top. "Is that for me?"

"Apparently." He held it toward me.

I took it from him. "Thank you."

"Sure. So, you live here?"

"Yeah. I just moved in today, actually."

"Huh," he said, rubbing his hands together, as if they were cold. "You know, I only live a couple miles from here. On Greeley."

"Really?" I laughed nervously. "What a small world." I had no idea where Greeley was, but planned on looking it up as soon as he left.

"Yeah. It's Chloe, right?" he asked, flashing me a panty-dropping smile.

I nodded. "Yep. Chloe Wilson. That's me."

Oh God, I sounded like a dork.

"I can't remember if we were formally introduced. I'm Graham. Graham Dodge. You can call me that or Dodge or even Dodger. That's what the guys call me at least. Dodger."

Was it me, or was he nervous too?

"The guys—as in the Gold Vipers?"

He grinned. "Yeah. Sorry. I'm actually a Prospect now."

"Oh. Well, congratulations." His black leather jacket covered the vest he wore, so I hadn't noticed any patches. And Jessica hadn't said anything.

"Thanks."

We stood there in awkward silence staring at each other for a few seconds, until he finally broke it. "Well, I should probably leave. Have a good night."

"Thanks. You, too. Oh, wait. Tank said I should try on the outfit. In case it didn't fit, you know? Do you have a few minutes? I can give it back to you if it doesn't work out and save another a trip out here."

"Sure," he said, giving me a funny look. "An outfit, huh?"

"It's actually an elf costume."

"Oh." He smiled. "Okay."

"It's for the fundraiser. I guess I'm handing out flyers tomorrow and he wants me to dress like an elf."

"Sounds like Tank. He really gets into the Christmas spirit."

"I do, too. Christmas is my favorite time of the year. Come on in," I said, moving out of the way.

Graham stepped into my apartment and walked past me. Taller then I remembered, he smelled very masculine, like leather and something else I couldn't quite put my finger on.

As if reading my mind, he apologized for smelling like exhaust fumes. "I just got done helping a buddy of mine move a bunch of cars around at the clubhouse. He was plowing the snow out of the parking lot."

"It's okay. I didn't notice," I lied.

"Wow, you really did just move in," he said, noticing all the boxes scattered around the living room.

"Yep. Uh, here," I said, rushing over to the sofa. I cleared off a place for him. "Why don't you make yourself at home while I go and get changed? Can I get you something to drink?"

"No. I'm fine. Thank you." Graham sat down and looked at the Christmas tree, which was still bare except for the blinking multi-colored lights.

"I just got that," I said, glad I'd put it up already. *It made the place look a little warmer,* I thought. "Just trying to make it more festive in here."

He nodded.

"Do you have a tree?" I gushed, talking too quickly. I couldn't help it, though. It felt so weird. I once again felt like a teenager, this time on a first date. It was so awkward, which I knew was silly, but all I could think about was the last time we'd seen each other and that kiss.

"No."

"Oh."

He looked away.

"I'm sure you're—"

"Busy. Yeah, I just… haven't had time," he said, looking a little uncomfortable. "Besides, it's just me anyway."

"It's just me this year, too," I replied, secretly feeling a little *too* happy about his admission. "But I couldn't spend Christmas without a tree."

He stared at me. "So, why are *you* alone this year?"

FIFTEEN

GRAHAM

*F*UCK. *SMOOTH MOVE, dipshit.*

Me and my big mouth. We were practically strangers and it wasn't any of my business. Fortunately, she wasn't offended.

Chloe smiled humorlessly. "You know that saying 'Two's company, three's a crowd?' Well, it used to be just my roommate and me. Then his boyfriend moved in and it just became too much," she confided. "Obviously, being the third wheel, I had to get out."

"Ah," I replied, a little relieved she hadn't just gotten over a rocky relationship. I didn't want to bring up unhappy shit for her. "That's too bad."

Chloe nodded. "More for Kai. His boyfriend is a selfish asshole who's using him."

"And he doesn't know?"

"I've tried telling him, but he doesn't want to hear it." She sighed. "I'm just waiting for the day Trey breaks his heart. I almost wish it would happen before the New Year, so he doesn't waste any more of his life with that jerk."

"I wouldn't wish a broken heart on anyone. Especially during the holidays. Take it from me," I replied, thinking about the incident with Bonnie again. She'd tried to reconcile with me many times, explaining that it was the drugs that had made her fuck Seth. Ecstasy or not, I didn't care, nor would I ever be able to get that vision out of my head. It still haunted me, even though Seth been murdered. Tank seemed to think the Blood Angels had something to do with it. His friend, Dom, the V.P. of the St. Paul Chapter, thought so, too. But, there wasn't any proof. As for the club getting implicated for Seth's death, no charges were ever filed. The cops had no evidence, and although they'd questioned the club, they didn't seem to think they had anything to do with it either.

"I suppose. I just don't know how to convince him that he needs to kick Trey to the curb."

"Do you have proof he's using him?"

"I don't have to. Kai pays for *everything* and Trey just freeloads off of him."

I shrugged. "He'll probably get tired of it."

"That's what I'm hoping. Anyway, I'm sure you need to get going. I'm going to try this thing on," she said, patting the package.

"Okay."

She disappeared down the hallway.

Settling back against the sofa, I looked around the room. Other than the furniture I was sitting on, everything else was packed away, so it was hard to get a read on her. Not that it mattered, I was just there to do a job. Still, she was definitely intriguing, and last year's kiss hadn't been forgotten. Not to mention, Chloe was even more gorgeous than I'd remembered. But she was Jessica's friend and I wasn't going to try and bang her. She was obviously a lot classier than the chicks who hung around the clubhouse. In fact, from what I'd overheard, she was a nurse and worked a lot of hours at the hospital with Jessica.

My phone began to vibrate and I noticed Tank was sending me a text.

Tank: *So, how'd it go?*

Me: *Good. I'm still here. She's trying on the costume.*

Tank: *Were you surprised?*

He had me stumped for a few seconds until I remembered Tank's mischievous grin. I wondered if he'd heard about the kiss we'd shared.

Me: *About what?*

Tank: *Chloe.*

There it was. He'd known and that's why he'd sent me in particular. I decided to play dumb.

Me: *Why would I be?*

Tank: *Fuck you. I bet you were shocked as all hell to see her.*

I chuckled. Tank thrived on drama and loved gossip. Hell, the guy was known to TiVo *Big Brother* and *Dr. Phil* for shit's sake. I decided to keep stringing him along.

Me: *No. Should I be?*

Tank: *She was the girl you kissed last year at the fundraiser. Remember?*

Me: *I kiss a lot of girls. Can't remember them all.*

Tank: *You're full of shit.*

Hearing Chloe step out of the bathroom, I put my phone down and watched as she stepped out of the hallway wearing the elf costume.

"I feel like there's been a mistake," she asked, smoothing down the short skirt.

I could barely talk. My mouth had gone dry the moment she'd stepped into the living room. The elf costume consisted of a satin red and green petticoat dress that accentuated her breasts, thigh-high sequined stockings, and a green Santa hat. She looked like a Victoria's Secret model ready for an "adults only" Christmas party.

"So, you're supposed to wear this passing out flyers?" I asked, standing up.

She nodded. "Apparently."

"I mean, it's *cute*," I said, watching as she tried tugging the bodice up over her cleavage, which wasn't doing anything but getting my dick get hard.

"I'm going to freeze my ass off," she replied, frowning. "He said it wasn't supposed to be revealing, but it barely covers my butt."

"Oh really?"

Chloe turned around, and from where I was standing, she was right. Her cute little derriere was barely covered by the satin material. I imagined her wearing heels and it was almost too much.

"You're going to be cold if he's wanting you to stand outside," I said, trying to nonchalantly adjust and cover my boner.

"Yeah. There's no way I can wear this with the weather the way it is. I'm going to call him back and see if there's something else we can do," she replied, walking back toward the bathroom.

"Good idea."

I sent Tank a quick text myself.

Me: *She tried on the elf suit.*

Tank: *Nice, huh?*

I could almost hear him laughing.

Me: *Too nice and too revealing. She's returning it.*

Tank: *I figured she would.*

Me: *Then why did you send it over?*

He sent an emoji with a wicked smile.

Grunting, I put my phone back into my jacket and waited for her to appear again. A few seconds later, she stepped back into the living room.

"Here," she said, handing the package back. "I left Tank a message. Hopefully he'll send over something else because I'm definitely not wearing that thing. It's cute, but not appropriate. At least, I don't think so."

"I liked it," I admitted. "But, I get you. You'd be freezing your ass off standing outside."

"Exactly."

Chloe's phone began to ring.

"That's probably Tank. I should get going," I said.

"Okay. Sorry you wasted your time."

"It's not your fault. Besides, it was nice seeing you again."

"You, too," she replied, smiling at me before answering the phone.

"I'll let myself out," I whispered.

She nodded. "Hello?"

SIXTEEN

CHLOE

TANK'S EXCUSE FOR the costume was that he'd received the wrong ones. He apologized for the mix-up and wasting my time.

"You're not the only one who contacted me. I don't know what happened, but I'll make sure you get the correct costume tomorrow. In fact, why don't I have one of my Prospects pick you up around two o'clock?"

"Sure."

As in Graham?

I wanted to ask for him specifically, but was too chicken.

"Great. I'll have him bring the costume over and drive you downtown where you'll be helping to pass out the flyers."

I imagined Graham dressed like an elf and it put a smile on my face. "Sounds great."

"It should be a lot of fun. In fact, a friend of mine, who works at the zoo, was able to loan us a couple caribou to use."

"Oh, cool."

"There will be hot cocoa, cider, and Christmas carolers, too."

"I'm looking forward to it. So, who did you say was going to be picking me up?"

"I was thinking of sending Graham back. Did he behave himself?" Tank asked, a smile in his voice.

Score.

"Oh, yeah. For sure," I replied.

"Good. Anyway, like I said… we'll send someone over, possibly Graham, around two tomorrow."

"Sounds good."

"Remember to call me if something comes up."

"Will do."

After hanging up with Tank, I turned on some Christmas music and went back to trimming the tree. As I hung up the decorations, I thought about Tank asking if Graham had behaved himself, and was a little disappointed that he had.

AFTER HANGING UP with Chloe, Tank smiled at Raptor, who was sitting across from him in the office.

"What did she say?"

"He was a good boy. Behaved himself."

"Bummer."

"He must not be related to you after all," Tank said, laughing.

"I'm a good boy." Raptor threw a pen at him and Tank ducked.

"You weren't when you were chasing Adriana all over town. If I remember correctly, you couldn't keep your hands off her, and she was barely legal."

"She'd just turned twenty-one. She was as legal as fuck."

"You mean she was legal *to* fuck."

Raptor chuckled. "At least I made an honest woman out of her."

Tank smirked. "That's 'cause you knocked her up."

"Fuck you. You know better."

"I know, brother. I'm just giving you shit. You were hooked the moment you saw her. I remember the night you two met. It actually was her birthday, if I recall?"

"Yep."

"Time sure flies," Tank said, staring ahead with a fond smile on his face. "That was also the year Frannie and Pops got married."

"That's right."

"I miss that son-of-a-bitch," Tank said sadly.

Raptor nodded. "Me, too."

They both sat there in silence for a few minutes and then Raptor cleared his throat. "You know, maybe Dodger's not interested in Chloe?"

"He's interested. Last year at the fundraiser, he not only kissed her, but after we got him hammered, he asked us to get her number, so he could hook up with her. You went home with Adriana, so you didn't see."

"Obviously he didn't call her."

"No. Dodger was trashed. We couldn't let him make a fool out of himself. Hell, he doesn't remember anything about it."

"All he remembers is how that bitch Bonnie hurt him," Raptor said, frowning.

Tank shrugged. "Oh, I don't know. He seems to have put everything behind him."

"Adriana thinks otherwise. She's good at judging people. You know, we've had Dodger over every Sunday since football season started. He usually stays for dinner and has been opening up more and more. He doesn't say much about Bonnie, but Adriana says she can tell he's not happy."

"We want him happy."

"Exactly."

They both sat there quietly, thinking. After a while, Tank spoke again. "Jessica raves about Chloe. I really think they could be good together."

"*If* there's still a connection."

"Unless she's gained five-hundred pounds and has grown a tail, I'm thinking they've got a shot."

Raptor smiled humorlessly and rubbed his forehead. "I can't believe we're even talking about this. We're guys. We should be encouraging him to sow his wild oats."

"He's been doing that, and apparently is still unhappy."

Raptor nodded. "So, what's your plan?"

Tank told him.

SEVENTEEN

GRAHAM

FTER LEAVING CHLOE'S, I stopped at the liquor store and picked up a case of beer. Now that my next few days were pretty much screwed with the shit Tank was signing me up for, I decided to forget the bar. The last thing I needed was to be hungover while playing Santa Claus. It was already a headache waiting to happen and I didn't need to add to it.

When I arrived at my apartment, I cracked open a beer, threw a frozen pizza into the oven, and walked into the living room. As I glanced around, I noticed how cold and bare it looked, especially without a Christmas tree. Even Chloe's place seemed more inviting and she still had unopened boxes sitting everywhere.

I scowled and took a swig of my beer.

Fuck Christmas decorations.

I was *not* going to waste time or money on a damn tree. For one, I didn't have enough ornaments, maybe a handful I'd made at school as a kid. For two, trees were outrageously expensive. Raptor had mentioned paying over one-hundred dollars for a real fucking tree. To me it was highway robbery, especially since you could only use it once. For three, I wasn't in the mood for celebrating Christmas. I felt like it had fucked me over last year and it was already biting me in the ass. The only enjoyment I'd seen coming was the snowmobile trip and now those plans were out the window because of the damn holiday. To make matters worse, I was being forced to dress up in a ridiculous costume and pretend to be jolly.

What a fucking nightmare.

Christmas was supposed to be about giving and spending time with family—and I was grateful to have found a new one. Even better, I now had the Gold Vipers, which should have been enough. But, it didn't feel like it. The truth was, I still felt empty inside and it was causing me to feel down-in-the-dumps. I wanted to shake it off. Tell myself that it was just a temporary setback. But I just couldn't.

I was too cynical at the moment.

I guess it was true about Christmas being one of the loneliest times of the year for many people. I would have never imagined myself being in that category, but here I was.

Taking another sip of beer, I pulled out my phone and almost called Bonnie. Fortunately, I stopped myself; as lonely as I was feeling, my pride was still strong enough to keep me level. One night with Bonnie and I'd be under her spell again. I couldn't afford to go down that road again.

I turned on the television and saw a holiday commercial with a woman who reminded me of Chloe in a way.

I sighed.

Untouchable, classy Chloe...

I wondered if there was a man in her life, besides her ex-roommate. It was hard to imagine a hot chick like her didn't have a lot of guys sniffing around. Of course, beauty wasn't skin-deep, and she could be very high-maintenance or have some hidden baggage.

I turned on a hockey game and told myself to forget about women for a while and enjoy my solitude. As lonely as it was, it was safe and stress-free. Some people would kill for that during the holidays.

EIGHTEEN

CHLOE

I WOKE UP around eight the next morning and continued my arduous task of unpacking. By the time noon rolled around, I had my kitchen and most of my bedroom things put away. As I was breaking down some of the boxes, my phone rang and I saw that it was Jessica.

"Guess where I'm at?" she asked, a smile in her voice.

"The hospital?"

"No. I'm downtown with some of the Gold Vipers. We're handing out *Meet Santa* flyers and hot cocoa. Even Jordan is out here."

"Is he wearing an elf suit?" I asked, amused.

"Hell, no. I am, though."

"Tank called me last night and it looks like I may be relieving you of your duties in a couple of hours."

"That's what I heard. I also heard Graham was at your place last night," she said.

"Just for a few seconds."

I explained why he'd stopped over and told her about receiving the wrong costume.

"You know, Tank was telling me that Graham is kind of a Grinch, which is why they're forcing him to play Santa Claus this year."

My eyes widened. "He's going to portray Santa?"

"Yeah. Should be interesting, if what they're saying is true."

"Huh. Well, he didn't seem very grouchy to me. He was very polite and cordial."

"He's always been very polite and we've had him over for dinner. I think it has something to do with the holidays, him being a crab. Anyway, I think Tank sent him to your place because he'd learned about that kiss you two shared last year. I have a feeling he's trying to play matchmaker."

Now *that* surprised me.

"Really?"

"Yes. I know you're a little scared of him, because of the assault last year, but I just found out why he went to jail and even I couldn't exactly blame him."

"What happened?"

She explained that Graham had found his girlfriend in bed with a drug dealer and beat the hell out of him.

"Yikes. That's horrible." And I couldn't exactly blame him, either.

"Even worse, he was going to ask her to marry him. He'd even picked out a ring that day."

"You're kidding! So, he was actually going to propose to her and instead found her cheating?" My heart went out to him. "That poor guy."

"I know, right? I can definitely see why he's not in the Christmas spirit. Anyway, I think Tank's trying to make the holidays more cheery for him by setting Graham up with you."

I was about to tell her I wasn't interested, but then realized it was a lie. I was more than interested. I'd been swooning over him since that kiss last year. Knowing why he was arrested made things much easier.

"I know. You're not interested, right?" she said with a sigh.

"I'm not interested in jumping into a relationship with anyone, but," I smiled, "I wouldn't say no if he asked me out."

She gasped. "Really? I can't believe you're actually coming around. You've been lonely long enough and he's so sweet, from what I've seen. Anyway, I'm pretty sure Tank is sending him over to pick you up later."

"He mentioned he might send him," I replied, looking at the clock. "Speaking of which, I think I'm going to take a shower and get ready."

"You go, girl. Oh, maybe wear some sexy underwear. You know, just in case."

"Very funny," I replied, but decided that it was good advice. One never knew, and usually, the best sex was never planned.

She laughed. "I'll see you soon."

"Okay."

NINETEEN

GRAHAM

"**Y**OU'VE GOT TO be kidding," I said when Raptor handed me an elf costume to wear. It was a green and red tunic with a jester hat and white tights. "I mean, dressing up as Santa is one thing, but now *this*? I'm going to look like a damn fool."

"Where's your Christmas spirit?" he asked, looking so amused I wanted to punch him in the face.

"What little I have is dying as we speak. Do I really have to do this?"

"Don't be a fucking pussy. Cleaner is out there right now, wearing one of these costumes and handing out flyers. He made no complaints."

"That's because he's going to be snowmobiling soon," I said. "While I'm stuck playing Frosty, the Gay Elf."

Raptor snorted. "Frosty was a Snowman. Not an elf. You should stop by later and watch some of the old Christmas movies with the kids. Get yourself re-educated."

I flipped him off and walked angrily to the bathroom.

Ten minutes later, I stared at myself in the mirror and wanted to crawl into the drain hole. Floating with the clown from the movie *IT* sounded like a better idea at the moment. The outfit was bad enough, but the tights took things to an entirely new level.

"You ready to go?" Raptor called, pounding on the bathroom door. "Don't forget. You've got to pick up Chloe and she's going to need time to put her elf costume on."

Inhaling angrily, I picked up my clothes, opened the bathroom door, and gave him a venomous look.

"Is the crankiness a low blood sugar problem? When was the last time you ate?" he asked.

Gritting my teeth, I walked around him and headed toward the doorway.

"He needs to get laid," said Hoss, who was now standing next to the bar with a smirk on his face. "Of course, I doubt he'll get his dick waxed wearing that."

"Don't be too sure. There's a gay bar up the street," Raptor said.

I turned around and held up both my middle fingers.

They laughed.

"Glad you find this amusing," I replied, opening up the door. "Merry fucking Christmas."

"Wait, you're forgetting something," Raptor said. He walked over with Chloe's costume. "Cheer up. Even the Grinch managed to find some Christmas spirit."

"He was tricked into it by the ghosts of Christmas Past, Present, and Future," I said dryly.

"That was Ebenezer Scrooge. Raptor is right. You really do need to brush up on your holidays," Hoss said.

No. What I needed was a stiff drink.

TWENTY

CHLOE

WHEN I OPENED the door and found Graham standing in the hallway dressed like he was, I couldn't help it. I laughed so hard I almost peed my pants.

"Sure. Laugh all you want, but you get to wear the same fucking thing," he replied, sighing.

I forced myself to try and be serious for his sake. The man was obviously miserable wearing what he was. "I'm sorry. I just wasn't expecting you to be wearing that get-up."

"Believe me, neither was I," he said, shoving a plastic bag at me. "Put this on and I'll meet you out front."

"Uh, okay."

Graham turned on his heel and stormed off.

"Wow, someone woke up on the wrong side of the bed," I muttered, shutting the door.

I opened up the bag and was relieved to find a velvet elf costume similar to Graham's, this one with long sleeves and thick faux fur on the collar and cuffs. He might not have liked it, but I thought it was cute.

Ten minutes later, I found him parked in front of the building in a big, black SUV. I got into the passenger side and we took off.

"So," I said, breaking the silence. "Tank mentioned there'd be reindeer?"

"Caribou," he corrected.

"Oh. Is there a difference?"

He shrugged. "I don't know."

I tried making a little more conversation, but he apparently wasn't in a talking mood. After a while, his sulking even began to affect me.

"Do you mind if we stop at McDonald's quickly?" he asked, when we were almost downtown. "I need some food."

"No. Go for it," I said dully, looking away. We hadn't talked in several minutes and I'd given up trying to lighten the mood.

He let out a ragged sigh. "Look, I'm sorry. I'm in a shitty mood and shouldn't be taking it out on you."

I turned and looked at him. "Really? I hadn't noticed."

Graham grinned sheepishly. "Can I make it up to you with an eggnog shake?"

"Good God, no. Those things give me gas."

"Nice. Let's both have one and pick up my brother. He deserves to get crop-dusted."

I laughed. "Wow. All this because of the costume."

"He ruined my entire weekend."

"What do you mean?"

"I had plans to go snowmobiling and he put the kibosh on it. Now I get to hang out with snot-nosed kids and overly-zealous Christmas fanatics."

"Wow. Thanks."

"I did *not* mean you," he replied, backpedaling. "Seriously."

"It's okay. I love the holidays. I'm not ashamed of being a fanatic. Heck, I wish I had a house. I'd decorate the hell out of it. In fact, I'd probably be the annoying neighbor with the blinking lights and loud music."

He smirked. "If it's the right kind, it wouldn't be that annoying."

"Probably Trans-Siberian Orchestra."

"No AC/DC?"

"I could throw that into the mix I suppose."

"Then I definitely would think twice before cutting the power cord."

"And what if I added some Ozzy or Metallica?"

"I'd throw a kegger and set up a bunch of lawn chairs for my friends to watch."

I smiled.

Graham pulled into a McDonald's drive-through and ordered a Big Mac, a Fillet-of-Fish, a large fry, and a large chocolate shake.

He turned to me. "You sure you don't want anything?"

"No. Thanks. I already ate."

After getting the food, we parked in the lot and he began to eat.

"Sorry, to do this in front of you. I don't usually eat in the morning and forgot to grab lunch," he said between bites of the Big Mac.

"It's no problem," I replied as I watched him shovel food into his mouth. When he was finished with everything, Graham looked content and in a much better mood.

"You're not diabetic, are you?" I asked, wondering if that was why he'd been so grumpy.

"No. Just an asshole who shouldn't take out his shit on other people."

"That's always a good rule of thumb."

"I'll try to remember it next time."

I thought back again to when he'd been arrested and wondered if he seriously really was a hothead.

"You and Jordan and Raptor really are brothers, huh?" I asked, changing the subject.

"Yeah. We're probably going to take a DNA test after the holidays. But the more time I spend with them, the more obvious it is."

"They both holiday Grinch monsters like you?"

He grinned. "Not that I can tell. It's our first Christmas together, so I guess I'll find out. Although, they both have kids and I think that kind of forces a person to be festive during the holidays."

"So, you're saying that once you have kids, you'll probably lighten up?"

"I'm never having kids, so I don't know."

"Never?"

"To tell you the truth, I don't care much for children. These days, most of them are self-deserving, whiny little shits."

Ouch. "They can be, but that's usually a parent's fault for indulging them."

"And society's fault for making it harder for them not to."

"Maybe. But, it still falls on the parents' shoulders to raise them to be responsible and not expect the world at their feet," I replied, thinking of the children I'd seen in the cancer ward. Almost every one of them were happy to just be free of pain and didn't whine about not having the latest toy or video game. All they wanted was more time, which was worth more to them than material objects.

"That's true. Another reason why I don't want kids. Trying to do that would be stressful and I have no patience."

"It wouldn't just be you raising them," I replied.

"Probably not, but I'd be the one laying down the ground rules."

"Because you're the guy?" I asked with a smirk.

"Honestly? Yeah. Women are generally too soft with their kids."

"Funny, I've heard many say the opposite. Especially, when a man has a daughter."

"If I had a daughter, I'd probably spoil her," he admitted. "But, I'd also become too overly protective, so she'd end up hating me in the long run."

"I doubt she'd hate you," I replied, amused. "She'd probably be as stubborn as you, though. I imagine there'd be a lot of arguing."

"Good point. Sounds like more stress than I'm willing to handle."

We talked more about his nieces and nephews, and with all of his talk about kids being 'little shits', he obviously adored them in his own way.

When we arrived downtown, Graham drove to the large park in the center of the city. It was decorated with festive lights, wreathes, and bows. Standing around a small, portable fire-pit were Jessica and a man I didn't recognize. Both were dressed in elf costumes. There was also a stranger tending to the reindeer, or whatever they were supposed to be, and two older women passing out hot drinks. I recognized one of them as Frannie, Jessica's mother.

As we got out of the SUV, I heard holiday music and saw a group of carolers nearby singing Christmas songs. It was almost magical and I was happy to have volunteered.

"Yay! You're finally here," Jessica said, giving me a hug. "It seems like I've been waiting hours for you to show up."

"We stopped at McDonald's," I replied, looking at my phone. It had just turned two o'clock, so we were still on time.

"Cleaner, this is Chloe," Jessica said, introducing me to the tall, burly-looking elf standing next to her, ringing a bell.

He smiled warmly. "Well, hello there. It's good to see more fellow elves."

"Hi," I replied, thinking he was kind of cute, especially with his dimples.

Cleaner looked at Graham and whistled. "Look at those legs. You must work out."

I had to admit, Graham's legs looked pretty muscular in the tights. Like a male ballet dancer.

Graham gave him a dirty look.

Cleaner laughed and shook his head. "Sorry you have to partner with Mr. Grumpy here."

Graham gave Cleaner the finger.

"Brother, there are children walking around here," Cleaner replied with faux shock. "Have some discretion."

Fortunately, there was only one girl about seven and she was too busy looking at the caribou to notice.

"Hi, Graham. Hi, Chloe," Frannie called out from the stand, where they were serving the hot drinks. "Come and get something to drink."

"I'll be right there," I said, smiling back.

"How's it going, Frannie?" Graham said loudly.

"Better... now that you're here," she said, giving him a wink.

"She's sweet on you," Cleaner teased in a low voice.

"Hell yeah, she is," Jessica said, smiling. "She's always like, 'Graham this' and 'Graham that'."

"She's a very nice woman and I don't mind running errands for her," Graham replied.

"She doesn't call you Dodger?" I asked, amused.

"No. She says she prefers Graham," he replied.

"She *definitely* prefers Graham," Cleaner said.

Graham elbowed him. "You're just jealous," he said in a lighthearted voice.

"Maybe a little. I haven't had any of her peanut butter cookies for a while and she makes the best ones in Jensen," he replied.

"They are good," Graham said with a smile. "I just had some last week. She put chocolate kisses in the middle. Damn delicious. In fact, she gave me a tin of Christmas cookies when I dropped off her groceries. Said I was her favorite Prospect and that she'd have more for me on Friday."

"You are such a cock," Cleaner pouted.

"You eat cookies with that mouth? Oh, wait. You don't because I'm Frannie's favorite now," Graham replied with a wink.

"Bastard," he replied, looking more amused than angry.

"Have some discretion," Graham said, throwing his words back to him. "There are children present."

"Okay. I'm outta here. I want to get packed for the trip up to Hoss's cabin. We're leaving early, by the way. Should be a blast, hitting this fresh powder with the sled. Oh, that's right. You can't go now," he said with a sly smile, patting Graham on the shoulder. "At least you'll still have cookies."

Graham gave him a murderous look.

"Here," Cleaner said, removing the shoulder bag he was wearing. "There are flyers inside and candy canes. Good luck and have fun. Ho, ho, ho."

"I hope your snowmobile runs out of gas," Graham mumbled.

Cleaner laughed and looked at me. "Have fun, Chloe. Maybe I'll see you around?"

I grinned. "Thanks. Yeah, maybe you will."

His eyes raked over me quickly. "You like snowmobiling?"

"I've never been," I replied.

"Perfect," he leaned closer. "I'd love to pop that cherry."

"Oh, Lord," Jessica said, rolling her eyes. "Cleaner."

My cheeks burned. "Uh. Okay?"

Graham, who'd also heard, gave a harsh, derisive laugh. "Smooth."

"Don't be such a sourpuss, Dodger," Cleaner said and then winked at me before he took off.

"He tries too hard," Graham muttered as the carolers began a new song.

"Some don't try hard enough," Jessica whispered next to me, a sly smile on her face.

I couldn't have agreed more.

TWENTY ONE

GRAHAM

I WASN'T SURE which irritated me more; Cleaner's jabs or the way he'd been flirting with Chloe. I also couldn't help but notice that she hadn't been offended by it either. As much as it shouldn't have bothered me, it did.

Let it go, I told myself.

After all, Chloe was just a friend. Hell, not *even* a friend. She was Jessica's coworker and not affiliated with the club at all.

Untouchable.

As for the kiss, it had happened almost a year ago and that didn't mean we owed each other anything. Still, it irritated me that Cleaner had pretty much asked her out, and knowing him, was already making mental plans on where and when he'd bang her. The guy was out for one thing and a woman like Chloe didn't need to be on his *piece-of-ass* tally. The last time I'd heard, Cleaner had bedded over fifty chicks and that was since he'd been made Prospect. I really wanted to convey all that to Chloe, but decided not to. As much as I didn't want Cleaner going out with her, we were bound by the club to look out for each other, even when it came to matters like this. I had to respect it even if I didn't always agree with what he was doing.

"So, what did you think about Cleaner?" Jessica asked Chloe.

She shrugged. "He seemed nice."

"That's because he wants something," I said, the words leaving my mouth before I could stop them.

"Well, he definitely wanted you," Jessica said, winking at Chloe.

Chloe's cheeks turned pink. "Yeah, I kind of got that impression, too."

"He's so funny and cute," Jessica said.

"Yeah," she replied.

My eye twitched.

What was so fucking cute about *him*?

"You'd better get yourself a tetanus shot if you plan on going out with him," I joked. "I'm just saying…"

Jessica laughed. "You two just never stop picking on each other. He was the same way when you weren't around. Actually, he was worse."

I grunted. "Sounds like *I'd* better get the tetanus shot. He can't seem to get me off of his mind."

Jessica and Chloe laughed.

For the next hour, we passed out the flyers and directed people to Frannie and Vanda, whom I learned was Raptor's mother-in-law. Meanwhile, Jessica and Chloe seemed to be having a blast, which had to be a 'chick' thing, because there wasn't any beer or food around to put me at the same level of happiness.

94

We were just running out of flyers when my cell phone began to ring. I checked and saw it was Cleaner.

"What's up?"

"I just found out I'm not going sledding either this fucking weekend," he said angrily.

Good, I thought. Karma was working in my favor for once. He'd given me too much shit about it and was now in the same boat. "Oh, yeah?"

"Yup. Tank just informed me that I have to help with the fundraiser, too. In fact, *all* Prospects are expected to stay in town and volunteer for elf duty."

"Seems only fair," I replied.

He grunted. "Fair. Yeah, probably. It still pisses me off. I'd packed and everything. Anyway, Tank wants us all at the clubhouse at six tonight. Apparently, we're going to take a trip to the nursing home over on Ninth Avenue to deliver some gifts to the elderly. Candy, popcorn, and shit like that. Oh, and he has your Santa suit ready."

I groaned. "Great."

"Is that hot blonde still there? Chloe?" he asked in a lighter tone.

"Yeah. *Why?*" I asked, an edge to my voice.

He paused. "You claiming her or something?"

"*Claiming?* No," I said, looking over at Chloe, who was handing out candy canes to a couple of kids. She was definitely hot, but too good for the likes of either of us, as far as I was concerned.

"You like her?"

My dick sure did. "Just stay away from her," I said grouchily.

"Why?"

"She's Jessica's coworker," I said, lowering my voice. "She works with cancer patients and shit."

"What does that have to do with asking her out? Seriously, brother, you sound like you're jealous or something."

"Do whatever you want."

"You're not interested?"

I didn't want to be. That was for sure. "Nope."

"Sweet. I'm going for it then, if you're not. She's gorgeous. Legs up to the sky and a nice rack. I'd love to see her in some heels."

I hung up on him.

TWENTY TWO

CHLOE

I WASN'T SURE what Graham's conversation was about, but after he hung up the phone, he was wearing his crabby pants again. I could see from his expression that something had really pissed him off.

"Everything okay?" I asked.

"It's fine," he replied curtly, avoiding eye-contact.

He had to be the moodiest man I'd ever met.

"I just received a text from Tank," Jessica said, looking at her phone. "He said we can pack it up and leave if we want."

"Good," Frannie said, walking over with two steaming Styrofoam cups. "Here." She handed Graham one and then me. "This is the last of the apple cider anyway. I have another cup with your name on it, Jess."

"Thanks, Mom," she replied.

Graham and I also thanked her.

"You need a ride home?" Graham asked, taking a sip from his cup. "Or are you catching a ride with Jessica?"

"Oh, I don't know." I looked over at her. I noticed she was helping Frannie and Vanda pack up their gear. "I could ask her."

"Don't worry. I'll ask her," he said.

Frowning, I watched him head toward the other women. He and Jessica spoke for a couple seconds and then she looked at me and nodded.

I guess that's that, I thought.

Graham walked back over. "She's going to drive you."

"Okay. I probably should have taken my own car. I hate being an inconvenience," I said, sounding a little bitter and regretting it right away.

He frowned. "You're not any trouble at all. I have to head back to the clubhouse soon. That's the only reason I asked about giving you a ride. But I'd be happy to take you home myself, if you'd prefer it."

"No. You're busy and Jessica said she would," I replied, embarrassed that I'd taken it personally. Of course, he had things to do. "I totally understand."

Graham looked relieved. "Good. I'm going to help Frannie and Vanda load up everything, so you two don't have to stick around."

"Okay," I said, watching Jessica head toward me, her keys in her hand.

"Ready?" she asked.

I nodded.

"Well, see you around," Graham said.

"Yeah. Happy Holidays," I replied.

His lips twitched. "You, too. See you, Jessica."

"Yeah, tomorrow actually. Tank's sending you guys to the hospital," she replied and winked. "Santa's going to pass out presents again."

Graham sighed. "Busy couple of days, apparently."

"They're going to our unit?" I asked.

She nodded.

Smiling, I imagined the looks on the children's faces when Santa and his elves showed up. "The kids will love it. What time?"

"I don't know," Jessica said.

"I'm sure we'll find out tonight," Graham said. "If you want, I'll call you and let you know."

"If you could, that would be great," I said. "I'd love to be there."

"What's your number?" he asked.

I gave it to him and he added it to his contacts list.

LATER, WHEN JESSICA and I were alone in her car, she smiled at me and shook her head.

"What's that about?" I asked, putting my seatbelt on.

"You don't see it, do you?" she replied, clearly amused about something.

"See what?" I asked.

"The way he looks at you. Graham."

My eyebrows knitted together. "What do you mean? How does he look at me?"

She started the engine. "With desperation."

"What?" I didn't get it. *Desperation?*

"He looks at you the same way Jordan used to look at me. Before we were together. Like a man who wants something so badly, but too afraid to go for it."

I laughed dryly. "Right."

"I'm telling you… he wants to get down your pants. Which isn't so bad, is it?"

"I think you're reading into something that's not there," I said, looking at her derisively. "Besides, I think I'd know if he had the hots for me. There'd be some kind of sign. All I've seen from him today is a rollercoaster of emotions. One minute he's up, the next he's down."

"He could be bipolar," Jessica said, a thoughtful look on her face.

"I don't know." I sighed. "He *was* a little angry about not being able to go snowmobiling this weekend."

Jessica's eyes widened. "Ohhh… He *was* looking forward to that. It must have been this weekend."

"Yeah. That's what he said."

"I remember hearing him talk about it at Thanksgiving. That was pretty shitty of Tank to take the weekend trip away from him. I guess it's all part of being a Prospect, though. Showing that you're willing to make sacrifices for the club."

"Well, it is for a good cause."

"Yes. A very good cause. Anyway, you changed the subject."

"I closed the subject. He's not into me."

"He wouldn't have kissed you if he wasn't interested," she reminded me.

"That was a year ago! Besides, he only did that because of that one gal. Candi, or whatever her name was. Seriously, Jessica, there's nothing there. In fact, we've been alone a couple of times and he's had every opportunity to kiss me again."

"I told you, I saw him checking you out more than once. He likes you. I'm willing to bet that he'll make a move, and when he does, it's going to knock your Christmas socks off," she joked.

I snorted.

TWENTY THREE

GRAHAM

AFTER HELPING FRANNIE and Vanda, I drove to the clubhouse and changed back into my street clothes and cut. Church wasn't for two more hours and I wasn't about to sit around wearing the ridiculous elf costume.

"Hey, you're here," Tank said, noticing me after he stepped out of his office. "How did it go?"

"Good. We handed out most of the flyers. I think there'll be a decent crowd of people Friday afternoon."

"Great. Did Cleaner fill you in on what I've got planned for tonight?"

"The nursing home? Yeah."

"Tomorrow we'll be visiting the Cancer Ward at Jessica's hospital," he said with a thoughtful expression. "I want to do something special for those kids. Jess is always talking about them and I can't imagine what they and their families must be going through."

I nodded.

"You're going to make a lot of children happy tomorrow dressed as Santa." He patted me on the back and turned to leave. "By the way, there's some wet meat and cheese in the refrigerator. And plenty of buns. Make yourself something to eat before the meeting," Tank said before walking away.

"Will do. Thanks," I replied, chuckling quietly at the term he used for cold cuts. It didn't exactly create a vision to make your mouth water, unless maybe you were gay.

I walked into the kitchen and made myself a couple sandwiches. Grabbing a beer from the refrigerator, I sat down and turned on the television. Finding a station with a hockey game, I cracked open the beer and enjoyed the solitude, which I knew would only be temporary. During third period, Cleaner showed up, and once again, began trampling on my parade.

"Hey, hey, hey. Long time no see," he said, grabbing a beer from the refrigerator.

"What's up?" I mumbled, sitting back on the sofa.

He kicked the refrigerator door shut with his foot. "Not much. How did everything go?"

"Downtown? Fine."

"Did Blondie ask about me?" he asked, twisting the cap off his bottle.

"You mean Chloe? No. Not at all."

"I'm surprised. I saw her checking me out."

I frowned. "You're dreaming. She was not checking your ass out."

"Maybe not when you were looking," he said with a sly smile. "But, my ass was on fire from the holes her eyes were burning through my britches."

"You fucking wish," I grumbled.

Cleaner laughed. "I'm just messing with you. Are you sure you're not interested in Chloe? You seem like you are."

"No, but I think you should keep your hands off."

His smile fell. "Why?"

"Because all you want to do is fuck her."

"What's wrong with that? She probably wants to get laid too. From what I hear, she's been single for a long time and too busy to date."

"Who told you that?" I asked, wondering why that was. Looking like she did, and working in a hospital, she could have bagged herself a doctor or some other rich white-collar worker.

"Tank."

"How does he know so much about her?"

He shrugged. "Probably because of Jessica."

Of course.

"Anyway, I'm going to try and hook up with her. In fact, after the 'Meet Santa' tomorrow, Tank's throwing a little party for us. He's going to invite her, and this time," he smiled wickedly, "*I'm* going to be the one giving her a ride. You know what I'm saying?"

Shaking my head, I pretended to get into the hockey game, but all I could think about was Chloe. Hopefully she wouldn't fall for his bullshit. She certainly didn't seem the type, but neither had Bonnie. Cleaner was right, though. If I wasn't going to claim Chloe for myself, then she was fair game. The idea of them together still pissed the fuck out of me.

"LISTEN, YOU GUYS," Tank said, staring at the five of us from across the table. "I know some of you had plans for the weekend, and I'm sure you weren't too happy with me when I changed them. Hell, I would have been pissed, too. But the holiday season is all about giving, and at the end of the day, it's what really matters. Especially when it comes to helping out our community. Tonight, we're going to take a quick trip to the senior home—"

"We should go quickly before the old geezers fall asleep," said Brock, one of the other Prospects who had a bad habit of interrupting people. "My grandmother is in bed by seven."

"Plus, we'll still have time to pound some beers afterward," Cleaner said with a grin.

Tank let out an irritated sigh. "We'll be leaving here in thirty minutes. The staff over at the nursing home wanted to make sure everyone had dinner before we show up with candy and treats," Tank replied. "And next time wait until I'm done fucking talking before you start yammering. This is the third time today, Brock."

"Sorry," he said, smiling sheepishly.

"Did you say Candi was coming?" Cleaner asked, perking up.

"Not for you," Brock ribbed. "At least that's what I heard."

We all laughed.

"Fuck off. I've never been with her," Cleaner muttered.

"Bullshit. I saw you leave with her a couple months ago. At the Halloween party," I said.

"She gave me a B.J. That was it," he replied.

"That's what *she* said when he unzipped," Brock said, making us all laugh again.

"That's not what your momma said," Cleaner volleyed.

"Okay, enough with the shit," Tank replied, although he too was smiling. "Candace isn't going to the nursing home. They'd lose half their patients to strokes. Now, let's talk about tomorrow and our 'Meet Santa' campaign."

For the next ten minutes we discussed what he expected out of everyone and the schedule we were to follow.

"Jessica and some of the other Old Ladies will be there as well," Tank continued. "They'll be selling some Christmas ornaments they made and picture frames for the fundraiser."

"What about that cute little blonde, Chloe?" Cleaner asked. "She going to be around, too?"

I sighed.

"I believe so. I'll have to talk to her again," Tank replied. "We could use all the help we can get."

"I'll call her up for you," Cleaner said. Looking at me, he wiggled his eyebrows. "Hell, I'll even give her a ride."

I could feel my eye twitching again. The guy just wouldn't give up. Was he *trying* to test me?

"We'll see," Tank replied. He looked around the table, his face serious. "Listen up. I don't want any of you meatheads making her uncomfortable tomorrow. She's donating her time, not her body. Got it?"

Everybody nodded.

"Okay," he said, banging the gavel. "Meeting adjourned. Let's bring some holiday spirit to the old geezers up the road. Dodger, I've got your costume in my office."

"Great," I replied dryly.

"Oh, quit being such a fucking Scrooge," Cleaner said, getting up.

"Yeah. He's right. Lighten up. Get laid or something," Tank said.

"Maybe he'll get lucky with one of the old broads at the nursing home," Brock said, chuckling. "Maybe you can 'tea-bag' an old bag."

The guys laughed.

"Oh, Santa! Let me see that North Pole of yours," Cleaner said, mimicking an old lady.

"Come and visit my chimney, I blew the dust out just for you!" Brock added.

"Sounds like some personal fantasies," I said dryly.

"You guys are sick fucks," Tank said, chuckling as he left the room.

"Dodger, can I borrow your Santa suit tomorrow night? I'd like to stuff someone's stocking tomorrow night, if you know what I mean," Cleaner remarked with a sly smile.

"Tank said to leave Chloe alone," I replied, glaring at him.

"He said not to harass or make her feel uncomfortable. I'm just going to put the old Cleaner charm on and let nature takes its course," he said.

"Charm?" I scoffed.

"Yeah. It works. You should try it sometime," he said with a smirk.

Sighing in annoyance, I headed toward Tank's office wishing I was on my way up to Hoss's cabin instead of to an old folks' home. Or in bed with a woman, now that I was horny after all the sex talk. An image of Chloe popped into my head, jacking me up even more.

Dammit.

Pushing her out of my head, I walked into the office.

"It's over on the cabinet," Tank said, staring at his laptop.

Seeing a large, plastic bag, I grabbed it and was heading back out of the office, when he told me to sit down.

"How are you doing?" he asked, turning away from his computer.

I shrugged. "Fine."

Tank let out a sigh. "Look, I know you're probably reflecting back to last year right now, when things were horseshit. Just remember that everything happens for a reason and you're better off without... what was her name?"

"Bonnie," I muttered.

"Right. Bonnie." He studied my face. "You happy, brother? I mean, *really* happy?"

"Sure," I replied.

"You seeing anyone special?"

"No. Which is cool. I'm not looking for anything right now."

He leaned back in his chair. "I'm sure being with someone like Bonnie has made you skittish."

"You can say that again."

"What do you think about Chloe?"

My eyes widened. "Why are you asking me about her?"

He shrugged. "Just wondering if there were any sparks."

"Nope."

His eyebrow raised. "Really?"

"Well, I mean… the woman *is* beautiful. Any guy would be crazy not to be attracted to her."

"So, what's the problem?"

"Are you trying to set me up?" I asked incredulously.

"No. I'm just trying to open your eyes up to some possibilities."

"Like I said, I'm not looking for anything, and if I was, I wouldn't be asking her out anyway."

"Why not?"

"Because. She's too… she's too nice."

"How do you know that?"

"I just do. I've been around her for the past couple of days. She's like Cinderella or Snow White or one of those other princesses." I imagined her singing in the garden, with little birds chirping along with her.

"So, if she was more like Maleficent you'd have no problem with her?" he asked, with a smile.

"She's just not my type."

"What's your type?"

I shrugged. "I don't know. Why are you so bent on finding me a woman?"

"I just want you to be happy and you don't seem like you are," he said in a thoughtful voice.

"And, you think I need a chick to be happy?" I asked wryly.

"Honestly, I don't know what you need. But, if you can think of anything, let me know and I'll make it happen if I can."

Feeling defensive again, I was about to ask him why it mattered so much, but then realized that it was just how Tank was wired. He loved his club and wanted the best for them.

"Thanks, man. I appreciate it," I said, holding out my hand.

He shook it. "No problem. Just do me one favor, okay?"

I nodded.

"Don't ever think that any woman is out of your league. And if she acts like she is, then that's her loss and your gain. Nobody needs a fucking snobby bitch. They never make anyone happy anyway. Too busy trying to please themselves."

"Point taken."

"And, if you like Chloe, or want to get to know her better, go for it. Just because she's different, doesn't mean it's wrong. Hell, opposites attract. I know more than anyone. Besides, you know what they say?" He smiled darkly. "A lady on the streets can be a freak in the sheets."

I grinned.

105

He grabbed a toothpick out of the box on his desk and stuck it into his mouth. "Now, go get your suit on and try to be jolly, will ya?"

TWENTY FOUR

CHLOE

JESSICA DROPPED ME off at my apartment and I changed out of the elf costume and into a pair of red, flannel lounge pants and a white T-shirt. Hungry, I made myself a grilled cheese sandwich and sat down at the kitchen table. It was made of oak, and very small, but fit perfectly in the small space. One of the other nurses had given to me; it was second-hand, but new to me, and in great condition. Other than that, besides my sofa and bedroom set, the apartment would be mostly bare. I had signed a six-month lease and wasn't planning on staying there any longer than that. Now that I was living on my own and renting, I'd decided to start saving up for a down-payment on a house. The less items to move, the better.

After eating my sandwich, I washed off the plate and was putting it into the dishwasher, when my phone rang. Seeing that it was Tank again, I quickly answered.

"Hey, Chloe, how's it going?"

"Great."

"Thanks again for helping us out this afternoon. We really appreciate it."

"No problem. Glad I could help."

"Look, I'm not going to beat around the bush—are you free tomorrow afternoon? We're doing the 'Meet Santa' thing and I could use some extra help keeping everything organized."

"No problem. I still have the elf costume. Should I wear it?"

"Yeah. Definitely."

"Jessica mentioned you probably needed help, so I was actually planning on being there anyway."

"Great. I'll make sure to get you a ride."

"Don't be silly. I can drive myself," I replied. Not that I didn't appreciate being chauffeured, I just liked my independence.

"You sure?"

"Yes. I appreciate you offering. I just think it will be easier for everyone if I just drive there myself. What time should I show up?"

"One-ish?"

"Sounds perfect."

"Also, I'm having a little party afterward, to show my appreciation for everyone helping out with this. Nothing too crazy. I hope you'll join us?"

"I still have a lot of unpacking to do, but I'll try to stop by for a little while."

"I hope you do. Anyway, I have to get going. We're going to be leaving shortly to visit the nursing home up the road."

"Oh, how nice."

"Yeah. Graham is dressing as Santa. I don't think he's too happy about it," he said, a smile in his voice. "But I think it will be good for him. I don't know if you've noticed, but he's not oozing with Christmas spirit."

"Yeah, I did catch that. Good luck," I replied, chuckling.

"Thanks. Before I forget, let me give you the address for the banquet room we've reserved for the 'Meet Santa'."

I grabbed a pen and paper and wrote it down. "I heard you're going to have him stop by the hospital tomorrow beforehand. The children are going to love it."

"Yeah. I'm going to have him hand out candy canes and small gifts."

"What kind of gifts?"

"Just, stuffed reindeers."

"Oh, how sweet."

"That's how we roll, darlin'. Gold Vipers have a sweet side that not everybody knows about. Tomorrow, we're going to prove it," he said with a smile in his voice.

I laughed. "Sounds like it."

"I gotta go. Thanks again and hope you have a great night."

"You, too."

After hanging up, I thought about Graham visiting the nursing home and hoped he'd get something out of it. As much of a Grinch everyone said he was, I had a feeling he wasn't quite as bad as they thought. At least, I hoped that was the case.

TWENTY FIVE

GRAHAM

I PUT THE SANTA suit on, along with the wig, beard, and cap. Although the costume was itchy and loose in the middle, it was of decent quality, not like some of the ones out there.

"Looking pretty swanky there, Santa," Tank said, when I walked out of the bathroom. "Where's the glasses?"

"They're in my pocket. I'll put them on when I get to the nursing home," I replied, patting the suit.

Studying me, he tapped his chin. "You need more girth. Nobody likes a skinny Santa. I'll be right back."

"Okay."

He walked away and returned a few seconds later with a pillow. "Here. Wear this underneath."

Looking at the pillow, I grimaced. "You kidding me? There's probably jizz on that thing."

"Nah. It's new," he said, chuckling. "Otherwise, I wouldn't be touching it."

I took the pillow, unbuttoned the jacket, and arranged it around my stomach.

"That's better," Tank said, after I had everything back together. "Now, let's hear some of your 'ho, ho, hos'."

Sighing, I did what he asked.

"How about with a little more enthusiasm," he said, his lip twitching.

"Ho, ho, ho," I said loudly.

Tank grinned. "Excellent. Let's go. I have the candy and reindeer loaded in my truck. The others are waiting for us in the parking lot."

"You're coming with?"

"Of course. Someone has to make sure you guys behave yourselves around all those gorgeous 'oldies-but-goodies'," he replied, slipping his jacket on. "Hell, Cleaner will probably add some tallies to his checklist of poontang if we're not careful."

I grinned.

WE ALL DROVE separately to the nursing home. When we arrived, Tank handed everyone else Santa hats, and then took out a red velvet bag. I opened it and saw that it was filled with small wrapped presents and mini candy canes.

"There should be enough reindeer inside for everyone," he said as I slung the bag over my shoulder.

"You sure they're going to want stuffed animals?" Cleaner asked, puffing on a cigarette.

"They're soft and childproof. I figured if they're safe enough for a toddler, they're safe enough for the geezers," Tank replied. "There's not much else we're allowed to pass out, anyway."

"Makes sense," he said, putting his cigarette out on the bottom of his boot.

"Hey, Santa, get your eyeglasses on," Tank said, looking at me.

"Oh, yeah." I pulled the spectacles out and slid them over my nose.

"There you go. You look good," Tank said, nodding in approval.

"He looks like he'd fit in really good here," Brock said with a smirk. "You'd better watch out, Dodger, or the staff might mistake you for one of their patrons. Especially with all of the diversity in this city. Not everyone celebrates Christmas and knows who St. Nick is."

"Three hots and a cot. Anything is better than last year, right Dodge?" Cleaner said, referring to my jail stay.

I gave him a dirty look.

"That's cold, even for you Cleaner. Quit fucking with him or you'll be the one in the Santa suit," Tank said as we walked toward the entrance.

"You're right. Sorry," Cleaner said.

I didn't reply.

We walked into the building and the attendant at the desk buzzed us inside.

"Oh, we've been expecting you," the woman said, smiling brightly. "Just sign in on the clipboard and I'll let the activities coordinator know you're here."

"Thank you," Tank replied, picking up the pen. He signed us in, and then a couple minutes later, we were led toward the nursing home's social gathering area by a woman named Mary.

"They've been waiting all day for you to arrive," she said, smiling. "This is the first time anyone has ever volunteered to do something like this, by the way. Thank you so much for making their holiday so special."

"We're happy to do it," Tank said, smiling back.

"Many of these people don't even get to see their family for Christmas. Some don't have a family." She sighed. "It's so sad how lonely some of them are. Your visit will be the highlight of their week. Heck, for the year for some of them."

Her words touched my heart, and for the first time, I was glad to be there.

"Get ready, Dodger," Tank said in a low voice. "Remember, you're Kris Kringle. You're a jolly, old elf who's happy to be here."

"I'm sure they know this is just a costume," I replied, smiling and shaking my head.

112

Tank grunted. "Jesus Christ, can you just not be so damn serious all the fucking time?" He gave Mary a sheepish grin when he saw her look back at him. "Sorry. Language. My bad."

"You must be on Santa's naughty list," she replied with a smirk.

Tank winked at her. "Mary, I'm as naughty as they come."

She laughed.

When we stepped into the gathering area, someone was playing Christmas music on the piano and almost everyone else was gathered in a circle. Many of the seniors were in wheelchairs and a few had oxygen masks attached to their noses. Fortunately, they were all wearing stickers with their names written in black marker, making it easier for us.

"There he is!" cried Ethel, an elderly woman with red hair and thick glasses. "Santa Claus!"

"Ho, ho, ho!" I hollered in a deep baritone voice, getting into character. "Looks like Santa got here just in time for the party!"

Most of them laughed.

"What he say?" barked out an old man named Ed, cocking his ear.

"He said he wants to party with us!" Ethel hollered.

Ed smiled and nodded. "Good."

"Santa! Would you like some cookies and milk?" a woman named Sara asked, shuffling toward me with her walker. "I bet you're hungry from that long trip from the North Pole. We have several kinds for you on the buffet."

"That sounds wonderful, Sara. Santa is always hungry for cookies," I said in a robust voice as I set the velvet bag down and opened it up. "But first, I have some gifts I want to pass out to all of you."

"What he say?" Ed hollered out.

"He has presents for us!" Ethel cried.

Ed grinned. "Oh, I like presents."

"Are those your elves?" asked another man, Bill. "Or your bodyguards?"

"We're both," Tank said, leaning against the counter with his arms crossed. He smiled warmly at everyone. "We wanted to make sure nobody stole any of Santa's presents before he was able to pass them out to you."

"Let me get some help from one my elves," I said. "Glitzy Sugar Pecker, come on over here and help Santa."

The guys all looked at me with confused expressions.

Enjoying this, I motioned toward Cleaner.

He walked over. "Glitzy Sugar Pecker?" he whispered, as I handed him some presents.

"Yeah. It sounds more elfish. Don't you think?" I whispered, chuckling.

Cleaner nodded. "I actually kind of like it."

"You would."

"I bet Chloe would, too. The sugary pecker part of me, especially."

I rolled my eyes.

We started passing out the presents to everyone and it was heartwarming to see the excitement on their faces.

"Can we open them?" Ed asked.

"Yes, of course," I replied.

"What?" he asked.

"Yes, you can!" hollered Ethel. "Open your gift!"

"Thank you!" he said, a happy gleam in his eyes as he began ripping the paper off.

"Don't be afraid to yell at him. His hearing aid doesn't work very well," Ethel told me.

"Oh, I'm sorry to hear that," I replied. "It must be hard for him."

"And for us. We're always having to yell at Ed," Bill said. "Makes my voice hoarse, if you want to know the truth."

"Here. Have another candy cane," I said, reaching back in my bag. "It might help."

"Thank you, son," he said, taking it from me.

"Don't forget to open your present," I said, nodding toward the box sitting on his lap.

"If it's a reindeer like everyone else has, I'd like to save it for my great granddaughter, if that's okay? I haven't been able to get her a gift for Christmas," he said, a sad look on his face. "I just can't get around anymore."

I patted his shoulder softly. "Be my guest, Bill."

"Thank you," he replied.

When all of the gifts were given out, I walked around and spent some time with each of the residents. A few of the elderly grabbed my hand with tears in their eyes, thanking me for just being there.

"I know you're not really Santa," a woman named Phyllis said in a low voice. "But, you made us feel young again. Thank you, dear fellow."

I patted her hand. "You're welcome, Phyllis. It's my pleasure."

And I meant it.

The longer I spent visiting with each of them, the more I began to realize how much I'd needed it, too. I'd been so self-absorbed in wanting to do my own thing that I'd forgotten how precious life was, how quickly it could pass by, and how lonely it could be. I even got a little choked up when one of the women thought I was her son, who I later learned had been killed on nine-eleven. Unfortunately, she had Alzheimer's and was confused. I let her think I was him, although I don't know if it was the right thing to do. But, seeing the joy on her face, I knew she'd needed it.

When it was time to leave, I was emotionally drained, but felt like I'd done something meaningful. In fact, I felt ashamed for wanting to skip such an important event for these people. Sure, someone else could have played Santa, but I was glad to have gotten the opportunity and had learned some valuable lessons. Ironically, I'd been the one giving the gifts, but had received so much more in return.

"Santa has to leave now," I said, waving at everyone. "I wish I could stay longer, but we're very busy at the North Pole this time of year."

"What he say about the North Pole?" Ed asked, looking confused.

"He's going back," Ethel yelled, winking at me.

"Oh." Ed's thoughtful look turned into a lecherous smile. "Speaking of poles... Next year can you bring me a doll, Santa? The kind you blow up and has three holes?"

Tank and I looked at each other and chuckled.

"What are you talking about?" Ethel asked loudly, looking confused. "Why would a grown man want a doll?"

"Santa knows," Ed said, winking at me.

Finally realizing what he was talking about, she scolded him. "Oh, yuck. You wouldn't know what to do with one of those things."

"Maybe, I should practice on you first," he said, wiggling his eyebrows.

Her cheeks turned bright red. "Well, I never," she said, stomping away.

"I know. Which is why I need me a doll," Ed said.

"Just stay on Santa's good list," I said loudly, winking at him.

"My clock is ticking. If I get a chance to be naughty, you'd better believe I will be," he hollered back.

We all laughed.

AS WE WERE leaving, Tank put his arm over my shoulder. "I have to say, I was pretty proud of you in there, Dodge. You took the ball, ran with it, and made a touchdown."

I smiled. "It was actually fun and hell, I learned some things in there, too."

He winked. "I knew you would. That's why I picked you specifically to play Santa."

I raised my eyebrow.

"I thought you could use a little Christmas spirit. You seemed to have found it in there."

"Yeah, I think I did," I replied.

115

He patted me on the back and then started dishing out orders for the next day.

As I was leaving the parking lot, I looked over at the nursing home one last time and felt a sense of peace that I hadn't in a long time.

TWENTY SIX

SIX

CHLOE

WHEN I WOKE up the next morning, I saw that it had started to snow again. Unfortunately, the forecast indicated that by nightfall, we'd have a blizzard on our hands, with record inches of snow accumulating. I'm not going to lie; I'm one of those people who don't mind snowstorms. In fact, I think they're beautiful, especially when you don't have to drive anywhere. Today was going to be a mess, however. I wasn't looking forward to driving in it and almost wished I would have taken Tank's offer of having someone pick me up.

Sighing, I switched off the television, made myself some coffee, and unpacked a few more boxes. At around ten, I had some oatmeal and fruit, and then jumped in the shower. When I was finished, I put on a pair of blue jeans and an ugly Christmas sweater, deciding I wouldn't wear the elf costume to the hospital. The kids would know right away and I didn't want them to start second-guessing the man playing Santa Claus. I didn't want *anything* destroying the magic he would bring that day. I had to believe that once Graham stepped foot inside of the Cancer Ward, he'd also want to make the moment as real for the children as he could. At least, I hoped he was that kind of man.

I dried my hair, curled it, and then carefully applied some makeup. Spotting the bottle of perfume on my sink, which was collecting dust, I put some on. I normally didn't wear any to the hospital, but found myself wanting to smell and look extra special for a certain someone, whether he appreciated it or not. As I was applying my lipstick, there was a knock at the door. When I went to answer it, I was shocked to see the guy from yesterday standing in the hallway. The biker named Cleaner.

"Hi. Remember me?" he asked, a warm smile on his face.

I gave him a puzzled look. "Yes. Sorry, I wasn't expecting anyone from the club to show up here."

"Didn't Tank call you? The roads are already getting bad, so I volunteered to pick you up."

"Oh, just a second." I hurried over to grab my phone from the kitchen counter and found that I indeed had a message from Tank. I walked back over and let Cleaner in. "I was so busy getting ready, I forgot to check my phone I guess," I said, smiling. "I told him I'd drive myself, but I'm glad you showed up. I wasn't looking forward to driving through a blizzard later."

"Don't worry. I'll get you home safe-and-sound," he said. "And by the way, you can call me Anthony if you'd like. Cleaner is my road name, but to tell you the truth, it's annoying as hell."

"Can't you change it?"

"Nah. The club gave it to me. They're amused by it, apparently."

"Why do they call you Cleaner, anyway?"

118

"I don't know. I guess because I'm always cleaning up after everyone. The guys are slobs."

I smiled.

His eyes flickered over me. "Anyway, are you ready? You look like a million bucks. Even with that ugly sweater."

Blushing, I looked down at my reindeer sweater, which I actually thought was cute and comfortable. "Thanks. Yeah, I just have to grab my elf costume for later. And my purse."

"Mine is outside in my Jeep. You know, we don't have to be at the hospital for another hour. Maybe you'd like to get a cup of coffee or have breakfast beforehand?"

"I just had something to eat and coffee, but we could get to the hospital early and grab a bite in the cafeteria, if you're hungry." The least I could do was treat him to breakfast for racing out here to pick me up.

He smiled. "Isn't hospital food supposed to be nasty?"

"It's really not *that* bad. Especially around the holidays," I said. "Let me go get my things and we can leave."

"Sounds good."

I put on my winter jacket and a pair of long, black boots. Grabbing my purse, and the bag with the elf costume, I thanked him again for picking me up.

"No problem. I figured you were getting tired of Dodger and his sulking."

I chuckled. "He is kind of a Grinch, huh?"

"Yeah. I think he might have found his Christmas spirit last night, though."

"Oh really?"

He told me about their trip to the nursing home and how, by the end of the evening, Graham had actually admitted to enjoying himself.

I smiled. "That's fantastic. I was hoping he'd have a change of heart about everything."

"He seems to. We'll see what today brings, though. Old people are one thing. Children are little shits and will surely test his patience. I know my nephews are handfuls, at least. They're always misbehaving and getting into trouble."

"How old are they?"

"Nine and eleven."

"I think that for Santa, they'll be on their best behavior," I replied, locking the deadbolt on my door. "Nobody wants coal in their stockings."

"You've got a point."

I turned around and Anthony was standing so close, I could barely move.

"Oh, uh, should we go?" I said, laughing nervously.

"Yeah," he said with a twinkle in his eyes. "I just have to say that you smell really good."

"Thanks."

He leaned forward and sniffed my hair. "It's days like this that I'm happy to be just a Prospect, otherwise I wouldn't be giving such a beautiful lady a ride."

Yuck.

I definitely wasn't interested. And his flirting was making me uncomfortable.

Forcing a smile to my face, I thanked him and side-stepped my way from the door. As I started walking down the hallway, he began to follow me, whistling "Pretty Woman."

I rolled my eyes and ignored it.

"Why don't you hold my hand when we get outside so you don't slip out there? It's very icy," he said, when we made it to the front entryway.

"I'll be fine," I replied, looking at the steps, which looked slippery, but manageable.

"Okay," he replied in a tone that sounded like I was making a mistake. "Ladies first."

I smiled and made my way down the ten steps in front of me without issue. Unfortunately, my boots had no traction. I ended up slipping on a patch of ice on the sidewalk instead of the steps. Before I went down, Anthony had me by the waist, saving me from a painful fall.

"Thanks," I replied as he let go of me.

"Told you it was slippery. Here," he held out his hand. "The last thing you want is to fall on your ass with those boots."

Reluctantly, I took his hand and he led me to a silver Jeep Wrangler. He opened the door, and then before I could protest, picked me up by the waist and set me down in the seat. With a twinkle in his eyes, he stood there staring at me as I turned my body and faced forward in the seat.

"Don't forget your seatbelt," he said.

Before I could pull it over my chest, Anthony was doing it for me, making everything that much more awkward.

"Uh, thanks," I said, trying not to lose my temper.

"Want to make sure my girl is strapped in safely."

I blinked.

Oh God.

"I'm hardly a girl," I replied, thinking out loud.

He winked. "Obviously, no."

After he shut the door, I let out a weary sigh and watched him walk around the Jeep and get inside.

"I'm going to warn you now," he said, starting the engine. "With the roads as slippery as they are, you're going to hear some language come out of my mouth you might not be used to. I'd like to apologize now."

"Hey, not a fucking problem," I replied with a small smile.

Anthony chuckled. "Glad to know you're not as angelic as Dodger thinks."

I stared at him in surprise. "He said that?"

"Hell yeah. To be honest, I think he likes you," Anthony said. "But is too chicken-shit to do anything about it. I asked him point-blank if he was interested, but he said he wasn't. I think he's lying, though."

"Why do you think he's chicken-shit?"

"I think he believes you're too good for him. Like you're some saint who might fall from grace if he gets too close."

"That's ridiculous," I replied, shocked that Graham thought of me in that way.

"I'm not afraid, though," he said, wiggling his eyebrows.

"Hold up," I replied, not wanting him to get any ideas and getting sick of the ridiculous lines he was trying to use on me. "You seem like a really great guy, and I do appreciate the compliments, but I'd like us to just be friends."

He gave me a pouty look.

I took a deep breath and told him the truth. Something that I was also admitting to myself for the very first time. "I'm already interested in someone else."

Anthony studied my face and then smiled. "It's Dodger, isn't it?"

"Maybe."

"It is," he said and laughed. "He must not have a clue."

"Probably not," I admitted.

"So, you two need to get together then?"

"I... I don't know."

"Of course you do. If I can't have you, then I'm making sure you get a shot with the guy you do want."

"What if he really doesn't like me? What if you're wrong?"

"He likes you. A lot," he replied as we pulled out of the parking lot, "Even if he doesn't know it yet."

TWENTY SEVEN

GRAHAM

I WAS STILL in good spirits the next morning, although I knew it was going to be a hectic day. Even the news about the weather being shitty didn't bother me too much.

I popped open an energy drink and was about to fix myself something to eat, when my cell phone began to ring.

It was Tank.

"Hey, what's up?"

"Just checking in," he said, his voice hoarse. "Make sure you hadn't forgotten about the trip to the hospital."

"Hell no. I'll be there."

"Good." He cleared his throat and I could hear him spitting on the other end of the phone. "Sorry. I think I'm getting a fucking sinus infection. I always get one this time of the year. Never fails. So, I'm not going to be there today. Wouldn't want to give any of the kids what I have. They already have enough problems."

"Bummer."

"Yeah. Raina claims if I take a couple tablespoons of apple cider vinegar a day, I'll stay healthier. That shit is disgusting, though."

"I take the pills," I told him. My adoptive mother was really into vitamins and I still took about eight different kinds a day. I usually stayed relatively healthy, but then again, I didn't have kids like most of the club did.

"She said they don't work as well. I told Raina if she wanted to help me out, douche with it and sit on my face," he said, chuckling. "We'll both be happy. She didn't find it as humorous as I did."

I snorted.

"Anyway, it sounds like Chloe is going to be at the hospital, too. Cleaner picked her up."

I scowled. "Oh?"

"Yeah. I was going to ask you to do it, but he insisted. She wanted to drive herself, but the roads are shitty and we're supposed to be getting a blizzard tonight."

"Huh." I imagined Cleaner flirting with Chloe like a motherfucker, and her falling for it. The thought of them together made my blood boil.

"You be careful driving, too. Better yet, take the sled and let Rudolph worry about the storm."

"Will do."

Damn you, Cleaner.

I wondered if I should say something to Tank about his intentions. He was the one who'd warned everyone not to flirt with her. Everyone but me, at least.

123

"You weren't paying attention, were you?" he asked, sounding amused.

"What?"

"Forget it. Look, the gifts for the kids are in my office at the clubhouse. More stuffed reindeer and candy canes. Could you swing by and get them on your way to the hospital?"

"Will do."

"Repeat what I just said."

"You want me to stop by the clubhouse and pick up the gifts. I heard you."

Tank chuckled. "Just making sure. Thanks, brother. Call me later and let me know how it all went."

"Sure."

"By the way, Raptor and Adriana are already downtown, making the space we've rented for the 'Meet Santa' program festive. They even made an oversized Santa chair for you to sit down on with the kids, so they can tell you what they want for Christmas."

I hadn't thought about that. I'd have kids sitting on my knee. Crying babies. Flashing cameras. And of course… Cleaner and Chloe dressed as elves, exchanging fleeting glances at each other. My Christmas spirit was beginning to wilt.

"Some of the Old Ladies are going to be selling ornaments, jewelry, and other shit, too. Sounds like it's going to be a real flea market. I'm actually bummed out that I can't be there."

"So am I," I replied. Tank had set all of this up and had been hyped about it for weeks. It was a shame he was going to miss out on his project.

"Raina is going to bring the kids, so at least they'll have some fun." He let out a weary sigh. "You know, I don't know how this snow is going to affect everything. At least the blizzard isn't starting until early evening."

"I think we created enough buzz about it yesterday that people will show, snow or not. Especially for their kids."

"Let's hope so. Anyway, I gotta go. Raina just walked in with a Hot Toddy. Call me later."

"Will do."

We hung up and my mind shifted back to Cleaner. He was obviously doing what he set out to do: bag Chloe. The fuck if I was going to let that happen.

Knowing I had to stop at the clubhouse now, I decided to forgo a homemade breakfast and pick up McDonald's along the way. Not something I really wanted, but nor did I want to be a hangry asshole later.

I took a quick shower and decided to wear the Santa suit right away, since I'd need it all day. Staring at my reflection in the mirror, I had to admit—I looked like a pretty buff jolly old elf, but knew it would change if I kept eating fast food and cookies.

As I was brushing my teeth, I heard someone knocking on my door so I went to go answer it. When I saw who was standing there, I regretted opening the door.

"What's up?" I said to Bonnie, who was holding a gift in her hands.

Smiling at my Santa suit, she held out the present. "I know I'm probably the last person you want to see, but I wanted to give you a gift."

I held my hands up in the air. "Bonnie, I don't want it."

Her smile fell. "Can't you just quit being a jerk for one minute? I mean, I've done everything to try and show you how sorry I am, and you won't even hear me out—"

"We have nothing to say to each other," I cut in angrily. "I mean, what in the hell do you expect from me?"

"Forgiveness, maybe? It is the holidays."

"Fine. I forgive you. Now... get lost."

Her eyes filled with tears. "How can you be so cold?"

Seeing one of my neighbors opening up their apartment door, I pulled her into my place. "How can I be so cold? You have the gall to ask me something like this after I caught you cheating on me last year, in *our* bed? I had to throw that thing out because I couldn't take sleeping in it anymore. I had to change a lot of things after what you did to me."

"I'm so sorry. It was a mistake," she said, moving closer to me. She grabbed the lapels of my Santa suit and stared into my eyes. "I still love you, you know. I always will."

I grabbed her wrists. "Stop it."

"But..."

"Listen to me," I said, trying to remain calm. I just wanted her out of my life, once and for all. "I'm going to be real here, okay? I don't love you anymore."

Tears streamed down her cheeks. "You're just angry still. I bet if we just gave it another shot, you' be able to forgive me and we could start again."

"We can't," I said softly, realizing that after everything, she might still love me in her own fucked-up way. But, I didn't feel anything like I had before she'd betrayed me. Not love at least. Looking at her now was like staring at a stranger. It was actually a relief.

"What if we just spent the day together? As friends. We can see where it leads to without pressure."

"No. I have plans today. Thus, the costume."

"I have to admit, you look kind of sexy in the Santa suit," she said, drying her tears. "Remember that time we role-played? You were pretending to be Santa and I was naughty, so you gave me a spanking?"

"Look, I have to leave," I said, remembering, but not wanting to. The very thought of getting together with her left a bad taste in my mouth.

"Could you at least accept the present?"

I knew if I did, it would give her false hope. "I appreciate the thought, but I can't. I'm sorry."

Bonnie let out a ragged sigh. "Fine. Just so you know, it was a bottle of Cristal. I thought we could have shared it on New Year's Eve."

"I have plans for New Year's, but thank you."

"With another woman?" she asked, her eyes filled with pain.

"With my family," I replied. "My brothers." There was going to be a party at the clubhouse, and afterward, Jessica and Jordan had invited me over to ring in the New Year.

"What family?" she asked, surprised.

I told her the news.

She grinned. "That's awesome. I'd love to meet them."

Knowing it would never happen, I didn't reply.

"So, there isn't anyone else in your life?" she asked, her smile fading.

I thought about Chloe, and at that moment, wanted someone like her in it. Scratch that. I wanted *her* in it. I just didn't know if she'd be interested in a scruff like me.

"There might be," I replied, honestly. "At least, I'm hoping."

Sighing, she stood up on her tippy-toes and kissed my cheek. "No matter what happens, I really do want you to be happy. Even if it's not with me."

"You, too," I replied, meaning it.

She touched my cheek and then stepped back. "Goodbye, Graham."

"Goodbye, Bonnie."

She smiled sadly and walked out of the apartment.

As I closed the door behind her, I felt like Ebenezer Scrooge might have on Christmas morning. After he'd been visited by the three spirits. I felt happy and content. I also had a giddiness in my stomach that had everything to do with Chloe. I'd finally closed the door to my previous life and was now ready to open a new one and take my first step.

TWENTY EIGHT

CHLOE

FORTUNATELY, EVEN WITH the roads being bad, Anthony and I arrived at the hospital early enough to get breakfast. After admitting that I liked Graham, he stopped flirting and I was able to relax. We ended up talking about the club and some of the things the Prospects were expected to do, without getting into too much detail.

"So, you guys do all the grunt work basically?" I asked, as he filled his tray full of food.

"Yeah. It's okay, though. Everyone had to do it at one point."

"Does every Prospect get patched as an actual club member?"

"No. There was one guy earlier this year who was always whining and just not keeping up on his end. It got to be so bad, that his sponsor didn't want to have anything to do with him anymore. Needless to say, he's long gone."

"How long have you been a Prospect?"

"Almost as long as Dodger. Ten months."

"Oh. How long do you have to be a Prospect before you're officially a club member?"

"There's not a set number of months. A year, usually, I've heard. The club has to vote us in."

"Do you think you'll be voted in?"

"I certainly hope so."

"What about Graham?"

"Dodger will probably get voted in because Raptor is his brother. He should, though. He and I are the hardest working of all the Prospects, as far as I'm concerned. We both volunteer for everything. I actually think he's trying to prove himself to everyone and not just get voted in because of being related to Raptor, though."

"Makes sense."

We found a table and Anthony began to eat while I sipped on my coffee. After a few minutes, a nurse I'd never met before stopped by.

"Well, well, well," she said dryly. "What are you in here for, Cleaner? AIDS test?"

"Ouch," he said, chuckling. "Amy, I didn't know you worked here."

"I told you I did," she replied. "Just like Angela and Karen also work here. You do remember them, don't you?"

"Of course. And… nice to see you, too," he replied, looking more amused than anything. "Did you want to join us for breakfast?"

"I'm working." She crossed her arms under her chest. "So, why didn't you ever call me back?"

"You never gave me your number, darlin'. I would have."

Amy snorted. "I'm pretty sure I did. But, hey, I guess I shouldn't have expected you to call me back. You didn't call Angela or Karen back either."

Before he could reply, she looked at me. "Do yourself a favor and don't let him take you home."

My eyebrows shot up.

"I actually have to," he said, smiling. "And we're just friends."

"Right," mumbled Amy. "You know, if I wanted a one-nighter, I would have used Tinder."

He just looked at her.

With a *harrumph*, Amy stormed away.

"Sorry about that," he said, dipping his toast into his eggs. "I meet a lot of chicks at the club parties. I get drunk and shit happens. It's not like I'm promising them anything more than a fun time, though. She made me look like a real asshole."

"Maybe you should be a little more upfront about it."

"Then I wouldn't get laid."

"Incredible," I replied, smiling.

"That's what they say." His eyes widened as he stared passed me. "Oh, shit."

I looked over my shoulder and saw another woman walking over to the table, a determined look on her face.

"This is not my day," he said, wiping his mouth with a napkin.

"Anthony, where in the hell have you been?" the woman asked angrily.

"I'll meet you by the Cancer Ward," I said quickly, standing up.

"Okay," he said and looked back at the woman. "Hey, Angela."

"Cancer Ward?" she said, her eyes wide. "Do you have cancer?"

I didn't hear what he said as I walked away, but she gasped. I turned around and saw her hugging him. He smiled and gave me the thumbs-up.

Rolling my eyes, I shook my head and went to find Jessica.

TWENTY NINE

GRAHAM

WHEN I FINALLY made it to the hospital, I put the rest of my costume on and entered the building. People smiled at me as I walked by, and I quickly jumped into character again.

"Are you really Santa?" asked a little girl who was just leaving the building with her mom.

"Yes. Some people call me Kris Kringle," I said, grabbing a candy cane from the bag. I looked at her mother and motioned toward it.

Smiling, she nodded.

"Thank you, Santa! Don't forget that I really want that doll I sent you a letter about," she said, taking the candy from me.

"I'll do my best," I replied, not knowing what else to say. Fortunately, the mother winked at me and I had a feeling she'd be getting her Christmas wish.

"Ho, ho, ho. Merry Christmas," I said before walking away.

After talking to a few more people, I went into the bathroom and called Cleaner to find out where he was and where we should meet. Unfortunately, he didn't answer his phone. I tried Chloe, but she didn't answer, either.

Frustrated, I walked out of the bathroom and asked directions. A couple minutes later, I was getting off the elevator and heading down the hallway to the Children's Cancer Unit when I heard a loud crash in one of the supply rooms, followed by some banging. I stopped abruptly and was about to open the door, when I heard someone moan.

"Yes. *Harder*," a woman ordered, gasping and panting. "Oh, Anthony."

"That's right, darlin'," growled a voice I recognized. "Spread 'em wider for me."

Rage burned through me as I pictured him fucking Chloe. She wasn't the woman I'd thought her to be. One ride from Cleaner and she'd dropped her panties like a club whore. Furious, I stormed away to find another bathroom. I needed to cool down before I blew up and ruined Christmas for someone besides myself.

THIRTY

CHLOE

"WHERE IS EVERYONE?" Jessica asked, twenty minutes later as we stood in the waiting room. It was after eleven. Neither Santa, nor Anthony, had yet to make an appearance.

"I don't know. The last time I saw Anthony, it was in the cafeteria." I opened up my purse to grab my phone and swore. I'd forgotten it at home.

"Anthony?"

"Cleaner. He said I could call him Anthony."

"What about the other Prospects?"

I shrugged. "I don't know. Maybe the weather is making them late?"

"Yeah. I suppose."

"Hey, hey, hey," Anthony said, appearing suddenly with his elf costume on. "What's shakin', lovelies?"

"Not much. Where's Santa?" Jessica asked, looking annoyed.

His smile fell. "He's not here yet?"

"Nope. Can you call him for me?"

Anthony pulled out his phone. "Oh, he tried calling me. I didn't even notice."

The elevator opened up and out stepped Santa Claus.

"Thank goodness," Jessica said, smiling in relief. "I thought maybe something happened."

I thought Graham looked so cute in the Santa costume. Unfortunately, he looked like he was in another horrible mood.

"Where are the others?" Anthony asked.

"I don't know," he replied, his eyes flashing angrily. "I'm not their babysitter. I had to pick up the gifts from the clubhouse, so I have idea what's going on."

His tone made me cringe.

"I was busy giving Chloe a ride, so I didn't talk to anybody else either," Anthony replied, typing on his phone.

"Yeah, so I heard," Graham said almost rudely.

Smiling, the other Prospect looked up. "Relax. You can drive her home if you want."

Graham looked at me as if I were a cockroach. "I'd rather not."

This time, even Anthony looked surprised.

"Wow, you'd better adjust your attitude before going in to see the kids," Jessica said, now looking very angry herself. "I don't know what crawled up your butt, but check that shit at the door."

Sighing, Graham turned to her, an embarrassed look on his face. "Sorry. You're absolutely right. Let's go. I'll be fine."

Jessica relaxed. "Before we start visiting the kids, let me go over the rules."

"Absolutely," said Graham.

As she began to talk to them about the children, I stole a couple glances at him, wondering what he was so angry about. It was obviously directed toward me, which was even more confusing and upsetting.

"Any questions?" she asked.

"Nope," Graham said.

"Nah. Let's go and put some smiles on the kids' faces," Anthony said.

"Follow me," Jessica said, turning around.

"Is there something wrong?" I asked Graham in a low voice as we followed Jessica.

"Nope," he said coldly, not even looking at me.

I decided right then and there that he was not the kind of guy I needed in my life. Handsome or not, he had more mood swings than I was willing to take on.

THIRTY
ONE

GRAHAM

A S FRUSTRATED AND angry as I was, Jessica was right. I had to check my shit at the door and give the kids a show, one that would put smiles on their faces and hopefully leave some lasting memories.

We spent the next couple of hours going room-to-room, visiting with some of the sweetest kids I'd ever met. Many of them were obviously very, very sick. Many had lost their hair. Some could barely sit up in bed and others ran circles around me. What they all had in common was reflected in their eyes. A kind of wisdom that went well beyond their years. Like they were old souls and knew something we didn't. Obviously, the cancer had a lot to do with it, and I could only imagine the hell they went through, especially when they were going through chemo. It was a very sobering experience.

"Santa," a little girl named Nora whispered from her hospital bed. She was only seven years old and had Leukemia.

"Yes, darlin'?" I leaned closer to her.

"I want to change my Christmas wish."

"Oh?" I asked, afraid she'd ask me for a miracle and it would break my heart. I could see that she was very sick and weak. I knew that what she probably needed, even Santa couldn't help.

"When I'm gone, bring Mommy and Daddy a baby. They wanted one before I got sick and I think they forgot about it." She smiled sadly. "I was supposed to have a brother or a sister."

Knowing what she had was terminal and that Nora probably wouldn't live to see it happen, broke my heart. I just stared at her for a few seconds, unable to speak. Here she was, so very ill, and wanted nothing more than to make her parents happy.

"Santa? Please?"

I forced a smile to my face and nodded. If I could have given her the world at that moment, I would have.

She smiled back at me and closed her eyes. "I'm so tired. Thank you for the reindeer and candy, Santa."

Sliding my fingers under the spectacles, I quickly wiped the tears from under my lashes, not wanting her to see them. Then I leaned over and kissed her on the forehead. "You bet, Nora."

I left her room having a new respect for Jessica and Chloe. They dealt with terminally ill children every day and I couldn't do it. It would break me.

"You okay?" Chloe asked.

I nodded. "That was the last child, right?" I asked quietly as we headed down the hallway.

"Yes," Jessica said and smiled. "I know, it's… tragic to see what some of these kids are going through."

"How do you do it?" I asked.

"Someone has to," she replied. "Someone who cares even if it's heartbreaking to be around."

"Do you ever go home and cry?" I asked.

"Oh, gosh, yes. All the time," Jessica said. "Ask Jordan."

I looked at Chloe, who'd been silent.

She smiled sadly. "I almost quit because of the stress. But, Jessica talked me out of it last year. I'm glad I stayed. Now I don't think I could ever think of leaving."

"It sure makes you appreciate things," said Cleaner, who'd been unnaturally quiet.

"You can say that again," I said.

"In fact, I would sure appreciate a beer right now. Do you think we have time to get a couple before we show up at the fundraiser?" asked Cleaner.

"You can do whatever you want," I said, although a beer sounded really good. "But, I'm heading over there right now. I don't think the kids will appreciate Santa having booze on his breath."

"Chloe? What do you say, should we grab a couple?" Cleaner said.

"No. I'm with Graham. It's not a good idea," she replied.

He groaned. "Come on. One beer isn't going to get anyone in trouble."

"You know what could, though," I replied. "Getting busy in the supply closet."

Chloe's eyes widened. "What?"

Cleaner stared at me for a few seconds and then laughed. "How'd you know?"

"You weren't exactly quiet about it," I muttered.

"Don't even tell me," Jessica said, giving him a dirty look. "You seriously had sex in the hospital? That's why you were late?"

"Sorry. It took longer than I thought," he replied with a sheepish grin. "And it wasn't planned."

I had a few things to say about that when my phone began to ring. I checked and saw that it was Tank.

"Hey, what's up?" I said into the phone.

"There's been a change in plans," he said, sounding annoyed. "With the weather conditions getting worse, a Snow Emergency has been issued for the entire damn city. So, we're going to have to cancel our 'Meet Santa' fundraiser, dammit."

"Shit. That's too bad."

"Yeah. Since you're already dressed up and have nothing else planned, I'm wondering if you'd be up for something else."

"Sure. What is it?"

"They're having a holiday sleepover party at the Church of St. Matthew for their students. Raina was telling me about it. Anyway, they were supposed to have Santa Claus show up, but theirs is stuck in Minnesota and can't make it now. You up for it?"

"That's the church by Eagle Lake, right?" It was about forty-five miles north of where we were.

"Yeah."

"Sure. Why not," I replied. "They were expecting Santa and shouldn't be disappointed."

"Man, I'm really fucking proud of you, Dodger," he said, smiling into the phone. "You know that?"

"Thanks, brother," I said, smiling. Hearing him say that felt really good.

"By the way, how did it go at the hospital?"

I told him about it, leaving out the part about Cleaner having sex with Chloe.

"Sad, huh?"

"Very. I have a new respect for Jessica."

"And Chloe. They both work in that unit."

My respect for Chloe wasn't the same anymore, but knowing what she dealt with on a daily basis was probably enough to make anyone make bad decisions. "Yeah."

"Why don't you see if Cleaner wants to go out there with you?"

I glanced over at him. He was laughing and joking around with Chloe and Jessica.

"Actually, I think I'd prefer to go alone." The last thing I'd need was to hear him gloat about fucking Chloe. He'd probably tell me every dirty, sordid detail and by the time we made it to the church, *I'd* be the one who needed to be cleansed. For killing him.

"Why?"

I made something up. "If the roads are bad, the fewer people driving on them, the better." It was a lame excuse, but it was all I had.

"I suppose. Did he ever pick up Chloe?"

"Yeah. By the way, Brock and the others never showed up."

"Oh, shit. I forgot to tell you they've been helping people get their cars out of ditches all day. Sorry, I should have called."

"It's no problem. When am I supposed to be at the church?"

"Any time after six. Try to be there before eight-thirty, if you can. Some of the kids will be sleeping by nine, I'm sure."

That meant I had time to grab a bite to eat beforehand.

"Sounds good."

"Thanks, brother," Tank said. "Call me later and tell me how it goes."

"Do I need to bring anything?"

"Yeah, actually, pick up some more candy or something. I'll pay you back later. Santa should probably not show up empty-handed."

"Will do."

"By the way, obviously, the party I wanted to throw for you guys is cancelled too."

"It's no problem."

"I'll make it up to you."

"You don't have to. Really."

"You know that's not how I roll. I'm going to show my appreciation."

"Whatever you want. I'm not going to demand anything, though. That's not how *I* roll."

He laughed. "I know. I gotta go. Drive safely."

"Will do."

I put my phone away and told them about the fundraiser being cancelled.

"That's too bad," Jessica said, frowning. "I know how important it was to Tank. Hopefully, they can figure out another way to raise money. They invested so much in this already, though."

"I know," I replied.

"It might be shitty outside but it's Friday night. Anyone else want to join me *now*?" Cleaner asked.

"I'm working, and obviously, I wouldn't anyway," Jessica said, smirking.

He cringed. "Ouch. Dodger?"

I told him about going to the church.

Cleaner chuckled. "Sucks to be you, Santa. It's going to take you hours to get out there if the weather is as bad as they say. Chloe?"

She shook her head. "No. I should get home and finish unpacking."

"Screw you all," he joked. "Party poopers."

Jessica looked at her watch. "I gotta get back to work. Thanks again, you guys. Be careful driving."

"Thanks," I said. "Say 'hi' to Jordan for me."

"You're still coming over for Christmas, right?" Jessica asked.

"Yeah. Definitely," I replied. "You want me to wear the Santa suit?"

"No, the kids will definitely recognize you, Uncle Graham," she replied with a wink. "They adore you, by the way."

"The feeling is mutual," I replied with a smile.

"Now we just need to find you a good woman," Jessica said. "So we can expand the family even more."

"You'd have better luck finding two identical snowflakes in the blizzard outside," I said, walking way.

"Where are you going?" she asked.

"I need coffee," I said, looking over my shoulder. Glancing at Chloe, I noticed she didn't look happy. Why? I had no idea. She sounded pretty fucking thrilled a couple hours ago in the supply room.

THIRTY TWO

CHLOE

AFTER GRABBING MY purse, and the elf costume from my locker, Graham, Anthony, and I rode the elevator down together. Nobody said anything. Anthony typed on his phone, texting everyone he knew about getting together. Graham just stood there, sulking for whatever reason.

Anthony groaned. "Oh, shit," he said, reading one of his texts. "My sister's in a fucking ditch and needs my help."

"Oh no," I said, feeling bad for her the both of them. "The roads must really be getting bad out there."

"Yeah." He looked at Graham. "I hate to ask, but can you bring Chloe home? I'd do it, but obviously, I'm going to be busy for the next hour or so. She has my nephew in the car, so I can't wait."

Graham nodded, but I could tell he wasn't happy about it.

"Thanks, brother," Anthony said as the elevator doors opened. "I owe you."

"Yep," Graham replied.

"See you, Chloe." Anthony gave me a quick hug. "Good luck with him," he whispered into my ear.

I snorted. I'd need more than that.

Anthony took off, leaving Graham and I alone together. I decided to try and make polite conversation, so it wouldn't be so awkward.

"So, where did you say you were going? A church?"

"Yeah."

"Which one?" I asked as we headed toward the doorway leading out to the parking lot.

"Church Of St. Matthew."

"Oh. Where is that?"

He told me.

"Wow. That is a long drive."

"Yep."

"You know, I could come with you and help out. I have my elf costume," I said, raising the plastic bag.

"I don't need any help."

"Obviously," I replied dryly and then sighed. "I just think it would be more fun for the kids if there's both an elf and Santa Claus."

He didn't say anything for a few seconds. "Fine. If you really want to come, you can. But, I'm warning you now, it's going to be a long drive and I don't know when I'm going to be able to get you back home," he said in a brisk tone.

"That's okay. I still have tomorrow off," I answered, wondering why I was willing to subject myself to such a crab-ass.

For the kids, I thought. *And Christmas.*

And, as ornery as he was, I hoped he might come around. Obviously, something was bothering him and not knowing what it was, was also bothering me.

"Should we grab a bite to eat first?"

"I was already planning on it," he said.

"Oh, good. I'm hungry, too. Where should we eat? I'll buy."

"You don't have to buy," he muttered.

"I want to. Where should we eat? A steak joint? Pasta place? Hell, I'd even go for pizza," I said, my stomach growling at the thought.

He gave me a strange look.

"What?"

"Built up an appetite, did you?"

"Hell, yeah. I haven't eaten since this morning."

He didn't reply.

When we got to the big glass doors, Graham whistled. "Wow, it really *is* coming down, isn't it?"

"Yeah," I replied staring outside. It looked like we'd gotten a foot of snow already and it was still coming down strong.

"I think we should just grab something quickly. I have a feeling it's going to be a longer drive than we think," he said, pulling his keys out of his pocket.

"Sounds good. Panera?" Hot soup sure sounded good at the moment.

"Sure."

I followed him out into the blustery snow, keeping my head down as we walked through the parking lot. When we finally made it to his SUV, which was completely covered in white, he told me to get in and then proceeded to try and brush off as much snow as he could. Unfortunately, it was coming down so much that by the time he jumped back inside, the windows were covered again.

"Brrr." He took off the cap, hair, and beard, and tossed the items into the backseat. The he began unbuttoning the Santa jacket. "This thing is wet," he said, pulling it off, along with the pillow he had strapped to his waist. "Good thing I put a T-shirt on underneath."

I stared at his biceps for a few seconds, remembering how he'd held me in his arms. Those sexy, muscular arms.

Damn him for being such a gloomy son-of-a-bitch.

He turned and caught me staring at him. "What?"

"Nothing," I said, looking away.

"You sure you don't want to go home?"

"No. I'm good."

He let out a weary sigh. "Okay. Just remember... I warned you."

THIRTY THREE

GRAHAM

I TURNED ON the radio, wishing I'd stuck to my guns and said 'no' about her going to the church with me. But she was persistent, and for whatever reason, really wanted to go. It surprised me considering I'd been so short with her.

Maybe she wanted to have a go with me, now?

I hoped not. I was the last person who'd want sloppy seconds. As attracted as I'd been to her—hell, I still was—just the thought of Cleaner putting his dick in her made me ill.

"What do you want from Panera?" I asked when we finally pulled up to the drive-through. What should have taken us five minutes, took almost twenty because of the snow and stupid drivers.

Chloe told me which soup she wanted and also asked for a warm cup of cappuccino. I ordered the same thing, along with a sandwich. After we received our food, I parked in the lot and we ate in silence. Fortunately, she must have gotten the hint that I wasn't in the mood for conversation.

When we were finished, I ran the empty containers up to the trash bin and then we were on our way.

"So, how did the nursing home thing go last night?" she asked when we finally made it to the freeway.

"Good."

"Did Tank mention if he was going to try and reschedule the 'Meet Santa' benefit?"

"I doubt there's time for that."

"We could make more flyers and maybe set it up outside somewhere? In the park, where we were yesterday even."

"It wouldn't work," I said flatly.

"It could," she argued. "If your club really wanted it to."

"Talk to Tank about it. See what he says."

She let out a frustrated sigh. "Fine."

I turned up the radio and we drove in silence for quite some time, going about twenty miles an hour. Traffic was jammed up and there were a lot of vehicles in ditches. Soon, we were barely going five miles an hour and it frustrated me so much, that I decided to get off on the next exit and try a different way.

"Why are we getting off here?" she asked, confused. "I thought it was much farther north."

"It is. I'm going to try and take the frontage roads."

"Won't that be even more slippery and dangerous?"

"Don't worry. My tires are new and have great traction. We'll be fine," I said, just as we hit an icy patch of snow and we began to slide.

Chloe gasped and held onto the seat as if for dear life.

"Relax." I pressed the gas pedal and regained control of the vehicle. "See, you just got to know what you're doing. Unlike a lot of other dumbasses," I said, watching another vehicle behind me spin out. Fortunately, they stayed on the road and didn't hit anyone.

"I still think this is a mistake," she mumbled as we turned onto the frontage road.

"You didn't have to come. In fact, I told you not to in the very beginning," I said tightly.

"Why are you always so angry?" Chloe asked, glaring at me.

"I'm not always angry. Some people just bring it out in me."

"Who? *Me?* What in the hell did I ever do to you?"

Look at me with those big, beautiful fucking eyes, I wanted to say. Too bad they were the same ones that had seen Cleaner's junk a few hours ago.

"Nothing," I muttered.

I was tired of arguing, and deep down, knew I was overreacting. So, she fucked another guy? We barely knew each other. Still, I'd wanted her to be different.

"Really? Because you're not acting like it. Or maybe you're just rude to everyone and I haven't been around you enough to notice."

"I'm not rude to everyone."

"Then why *me?*"

I clenched my teeth together, not wanting to admit to her that I was jealous. It was hard enough to admit to myself.

"You're a real peach," she muttered, looking out her side window. "And you're right. I shouldn't have taken this trip with you. I just thought… I don't know what I thought, actually."

Instead of replying, I changed the radio station and turned up a song I liked. We continued on the frontage road and then got onto another. As we drove, I glanced over and noticed Chloe had drifted off.

Thank God.

After a few more miles, the frontage road ended and I was faced with going west or east.

"Where are we?" she asked drowsily, opening her eyes and sitting up.

"Almost there," I said, taking a right, hoping we were heading back toward the highway. I didn't recognize the name of the street we were currently on, but I didn't get out that way very often. Hell, I'd only been to the church once.

Her eyebrows knitted together. "Almost? As in a couple more miles?"

"Not sure," I admitted.

"Maybe you should check Google Maps," she suggested.

Sighing, I took out my cell and was about to do just that when Chloe yelled at me about driving while using my phone.

"Relax. I do it all the time."

"I'm sure, but the roads are slipperier than hell," Chloe snapped. "I'd like to live to see Christmas."

"Fine. *You* check it for me," I said, typing in my passcode before handing my phone to her.

"I don't know if you noticed, but your phone is almost dead," she said, swiping the screen to find the internet browser.

"Then hurry up."

She gave an exasperated sigh. "Oh, crap. There it goes. It's totally dead now. Do you have a charger in here?"

"I should. Check the glove compartment."

She opened it up and began digging around. "I don't see one."

Remembering I'd taken it out, I groaned and told her.

She closed the glovebox. "Now what?"

"Where's your phone?" I asked.

"I forgot it at home."

I sighed. "Great."

"Why don't we stop at the next gas station and ask for directions?"

"I guess we'll have to."

THIRTY FOUR

CHLOE

IT WAS ANOTHER twenty minutes before were able to get to a gas station. They didn't have any phone chargers, but we did learn from one of the attendants that we weren't too far from the church.

"And you doubted me," Graham said, as we started driving again.

"I never doubted your ability to find the church. I just doubted your driving skills," I admitted.

"Ha. Funny," he said dryly.

I looked at him. "Do you see me laughing?"

WHEN WE FINALLY reached the church, it was almost seven o'clock. Most of the lights were off and there were only a couple of cars in the parking lot, and they were almost buried in snow.

"This doesn't look good," Graham said, frowning. "Wait here. I'm going to see what's going on." He reached into the back, grabbing the Santa jacket, hat, and hair pieces again. "I'd better put on everything, in case one of the kids see me."

"Good idea."

He quickly got dressed and then left me in the truck. A few minutes later, he returned, looking even more aggravated.

"What's wrong now?"

"They canceled the overnight," he grumbled, slamming the door shut. "We wasted a trip out here."

"Damn. I wonder if Tank tried calling you?"

"I have no idea, obviously. My phone is dead." Graham ripped off the hat and hair pieces. "I seriously need a fucking drink after all of this."

"You want to stop somewhere? I could go for something myself," I admitted.

Not saying anything, he drove off the parking lot and began turned back from where we came. Instead of getting back onto the frontage road, however, he kept going.

"Where are we going?"

"You wanted a drink," he said firmly. "We're going to find a place to have one."

"You wanted one, too," I replied, not wanting him to think it was all my idea.

"I said I *needed* a drink. There's a difference."

Oh, my God.

I wanted to smack him. He was so damn infuriating. Everything had to be an argument. As angry as I was, I didn't take the bait. He was obviously looking for an argument.

About a mile up the road, we pulled into the parking lot of a shabby-looking bar named "Dan's Dive." Despite the weather conditions, there were a lot of vehicles in the lot.

"Have you ever been here before?"

"Yeah. I went to a wedding reception here once."

"Wow. I can't believe it's so busy," I said, shocked.

"It's Friday night and there's not much else to do in these parts," he replied, pulling off his Santa cap. "But drink."

"Apparently," I replied.

He parked the SUV and then proceeded to take the top half of his costume off again, leaving only the jacket, pants, and boots.

We both got out, and fortunately, a couple men were snow-blowing the parking lot and sidewalks, so we had a clear path to the front door. When we stepped inside the bar, there was a band playing country music in back.

"This is why it's so busy," Graham said, staring at the band.

"I love live music," I said, stomping the snow off my boots.

"I'd say let's sit at the bar, but it's jam-packed," he said, scanning the area with a perturbed look on his face.

"There's a place over there," I said, pointing near the stage. Two people were just walking away from a round pub table with their coats on. "We'd better get it before someone else does."

Graham took off toward it and I followed him through a crowd of people. Fortunately, we were able to claim the table right before another couple.

"What do you want?" he asked as I sat down on one of the chairs. "I'll go get us a couple of drinks."

"Um, a Bloody Mary?"

"Spicy?"

"Yeah."

"A chaser?"

"Sure."

"You still like those, huh?" he asked.

"It's my favorite drink," I replied, thinking he must have remembered Jessica making me one the time we'd met. I was surprised.

"I'll be right back," he said and walked away.

Sighing, I took off my jacket, sat back in the chair, and stared at the stage. Although I wasn't much for country music, I had to admit the singer had a great voice. I wasn't the only one who thought so, because several women were dancing and staring at him like they wanted to take him home. Of course, it didn't hurt that he was good looking.

"No fucking way," said a voice I recognized. One that gave me the chills. "As I live and breathe. Chloe, damn… it's a small world."

Turning to Brent, my ex-boyfriend—the very last person I wanted to run into *ever*—I forced a smile to my face. "Hi."

Without even asking, he sat down in the empty chair across from me. "You're looking as foxy as ever, save for the ugly Christmas sweater. What are you doing way out here, gorgeous?"

"I'm here with a friend."

His grinned widened. "Kai?"

"No. Someone else."

Graham appeared at the table. He set my Bloody Mary down in front of me, along with the chaser.

"Thank you," I said.

"You're welcome," he said.

Brent looked up at him with scorn. "Well, look who we have here? Santa Claus. Or, are you one of his little elves?"

Graham smiled down at him coolly. "Little? Now, that's one thing I've never been called by a chick before. What did you say your name was, darlin'?"

"Darlin'?" Brent's entire face turned red as the rage kicked in. "You think you're funny?" He stood up, and to my amusement, the top of his head only came to Graham's nose. "You're just a rude asshole trying to impress Chloe here."

Graham's eye twitched. "I don't have to impress anyone. If I did, you'd already be on the floor crying for your mama."

Before I could try and defuse the situation, another man showed up at the table.

"Graham Dodge? Is that you?" the stranger asked, giving him a friendly smile.

Graham's entire face changed. He grinned warmly at the other guy and held out his hand. "Matt Davis. Holy shit. I haven't seen you since high school. What are you doing here?"

"Just enjoying the music," he replied, shaking it.

"You always did like country," Graham said as Brent slipped away, still glaring at him.

"And you don't, which is why I wouldn't have thought I'd ever see you here. Speaking of which, what was happening with that douchebag? You two looked like you were going to get into a fight there for a second," he answered.

"I don't know. He was just being a dick. Short-man syndrome, you know?" Graham said, taking a swig of his beer.

Matt looked at me. "Aren't you going to introduce me to your girl?"

"This is Chloe," Graham said. "And… she's not my girl."

"Hi," I said, not knowing whether to laugh or cry. The way Graham had introduced me was borderline cruel. Even Tim looked a little surprised.

"Hi. Nice to meet you."

"You, too," I said.

He looked back at Graham. "So, you married yet or have any kids?"

"No."

"That's cool. Nothing wrong with that. Anyway, we should get together and have a beer soon. I'm with my wife right now and she's going to kill me if I don't get back soon. It's our anniversary. I just had to see if it was really you."

"Happy anniversary. Here." Graham pulled out his wallet and took out a business card. "Call me. I'd love to hook up."

"Master Electrician. Good to know," Matt said, putting the card in his shirt pocket. "I'm thinking of buying a cabin and might need some advice on a few things."

"I'll be happy to help," Graham replied.

"Sweet." Matt nodded at me. "Have a good night, Chloe."

"You, too," I replied.

After Matt walked away, Graham sat down across from me. "What was that dickhead saying to you before I arrived?"

"Brent?"

His eyebrow arched. "Oh, you know him?"

"He's an ex-boyfriend. A real asshole, by the way. I'm glad you got rid of him," I replied, noticing Brent watching me from another table. He was with two other guys, obviously talking about what had transpired. I recognized one of them and remembered him being a troublemaker.

"How long ago did you date him?"

"It's been almost two years," I replied.

"He's obviously still interested in you," Graham said, taking another drink of his beer.

"I hope not. Anyway, maybe we should drink up quickly and get out of here," I said, noticing that Brent's friends looked almost like they were sizing Graham up. "I don't want anything to happen."

"You afraid of him?"

I looked at Graham and nodded. "He's the kind of guy who'll wait for you out in the parking lot and get you from behind."

"Is that right?" he replied and looked at Brent. "So, you're saying I shouldn't have pissed him off?"

"Probably not," I replied. "He's angrier than hell now. You made him look like a fool."

"He did that too himself," Graham replied.

I began drinking my Bloody Mary faster. I really wanted to get out of there. I knew something was going to happen if we didn't leave.

"Hey, take your time. We're not in a hurry and I'm certainly not going to let him bother us."

I forced myself to relax. At least Graham was being nicer to me. That was a plus. "Okay."

The song ended and a new one began. It was slow and steady. Several couples got onto the dance floor.

"You want to dance?" Graham asked, shocking the hell out of me.

THIRTY FIVE

GRAHAM

I KNEW I was playing with fire, in more ways than one, but couldn't help it. I was in a punchy mood and looking to take my frustrations out on Chloe's ex, who was giving me the stink eye. Sure, I could have ignored him, but I decided pushing him further would be much more fun.

"Dance? You want to *dance*?" Chloe said shocked.

"Yeah. I like this song."

She studied my face. "I bet you've never even heard it."

"So? I still like it," I replied, holding out my hand.

Chloe drank the rest of her Bloody Mary and then set the glass down. We walked out onto the dance floor and I pulled her into my arms. She felt so good, her body pressed against mine; I immediately knew I'd made a mistake.

"You're a good dancer," she said after a while. "Do you do this kind of thing a lot?"

"Dance? No."

"I would have never guessed," she said, pressing her cheek against my chest. "This feels nice."

"You smell nice," I murmured, inhaling her perfume. I'd missed it in the truck, but now that her coat was off, the scent was noticeable.

"Thanks," she whispered.

Closing my eyes, I continued dancing with Chloe, trying to enjoy the moment and wishing things were different. Wishing *I'd* been the one who'd given her a ride to the hospital earlier. Just maybe... she wouldn't have ended up in the supply room with Cleaner.

I sighed.

After everything, it was frustrating to know how much I still wanted her. And from the boner pressed against her, she probably realized it, too.

THIRTY SIX

CHLOE

I T FELT SO good being in Graham's strong arms. Not only was he smooth on his feet, but we seemed to fit together perfectly. And if that wasn't enough to get my lady-parts all hot and bothered, I could tell that I wasn't the only one enjoying it.

I closed my eyes and pressed my hips closer to his, wondering why I always fell for the wrong kind of guys. Graham was moody, cynical, and exasperating. He was also as confusing as a Rubik's Cube. Just when I thought I had him figured out, I… didn't. It was maddening.

But there was no denying he wanted me. I just didn't understand why he was so damn angry. As far as I could tell, I hadn't done anything to piss him off. I wondered if he had some kind of mental psychosis. I hoped it wasn't the case; I was aching to have sex with him, and if it happened by some miracle, I didn't want to find out that he was unhinged. Watching him earlier with Brent, I could see how badly Graham had itched to fight him. He'd been practically salivating at the chance. It even made me wonder if Graham's excitement stemmed from the thought of beating Brent to a pulp.

No.

He hadn't been hard until we'd started dancing. I was sure of that.

Feeling slightly buzzed and more courageous than usual, I stole a glance at his lips and wondered what he'd do if I kissed him. I wanted to badly, and yet, I also didn't want to be rejected. His current mood was unpredictable, I had no idea how he'd react. He could freak out.

Suddenly, I felt his hands lower to my hips, pulling me even closer to his erection.

Or maybe he wouldn't freak out…

He began caressing my butt. The sensation caused an ache of desire between my legs so strong, they grew weak. Afraid to break the spell, I stayed pliable in his arms, moving with the music and wondering how far he would take this. Just as I was starting to get up enough nerve to begin my own exploration, he tilted my chin up to his face and kissed me. Shaking with need, I kissed him back with everything I had.

Graham groaned in the back of his throat and suddenly, I could feel him pulling me away from the dance floor. He raised his face from mine and stared down at me with hunger.

"You want to get out of here?" he asked, huskily.

I nodded.

"Come on."

He led me back to the table, grabbed my jacket, and pulled me through the bar. Instead of walking out the front door, however, he took me down a different hallway, obviously not meant for customers, to a staircase.

"Are we supposed to be down here?" I asked as we walked down the steps, nervous we were going to get into trouble.

"Probably not," he said in a low voice. "Watch your step."

It was dark at the bottom of the staircase; we couldn't see anything at all. Holding my hand, he pulled me with him.

"Where are we going?" I whispered, my heart racing.

In answer, he stopped and pushed me up against the wall. Suddenly, he was kissing me so hard, it almost hurt. His hands moved to my breasts, squeezing them roughly through my sweater, my moans a mixture of desire and pain.

"Wait," I whispered when his lips left mine and he was fumbling with the buttons on my jeans.

"For what?"

"I… Oh, God," I moaned as he slid his hand down to my panties, which were wet.

Touching the thin fabric, he froze. "Tell me he used a rubber," he growled.

I didn't understand. "What?"

"Cleaner." Groaning, he moved his hand away. "I can't do this. What the fuck am I even thinking?"

"Wait a second, did you just ask me if Cleaner used a rubber? With *me*?" I asked, shocked.

"Yeah. I hope he did. For your sake," he said in a scornful tone.

"I have *never* had sex with Anthony," I said angrily. "Where in the hell did you get that idea?"

"Right. Did you already forget about the supply room at the hospital? Don't even fucking deny it; I heard the two of you," he snapped back.

I let out an angry growl and zipped my jeans back up. I couldn't believe he was accusing me of this. "Look, I don't know what you heard, but it certainly wasn't me!"

"Then who was it? Some random chick he met at the hospital the short time he was there? Cleaner is good, but he's not *that* good."

"You know," I said, laughing coldly. "If you think he's so good, why don't you go and fuck him yourself? Let me know if it's everything you imagined it to be."

The lights suddenly turned on and a man stood there, glaring at us. "Listen, you two. This isn't open to the public. I don't care who either of you fuck, as long as it's not here in my basement!"

THIRTY SEVEN

GRAHAM

A FTER APOLOGIZING TO the owner, I followed Chloe up the steps and out to the parking lot. She was so angry, she refused to even look at me. Realizing I must have made a mistake, I felt like the worst asshole ever.

"I'm sorry," I said, trying to grab her hand. "Honest to God, I really thought it was you he was having sex with. It's… it's why I was such a dick to you all night."

She stopped in her tracks and turned to me, looking even more furious. "Really? *That's* why? Did it ever occur to you that I'm not a fucking slut who would have sex with just anyone?" Her eyes grew wider. "Or, maybe you did and that's why you brought me to the basement. To have a shot at me, too?"

"Chloe, I'm sorry," I repeated, reaching for her. She was right, though. I *had* dragged her down there intentionally. But, I'd wanted her so fucking badly. Even after believing that one of my club brothers had gotten to her before me. That's how pathetic I was. I felt like such a shit for so many reasons.

"*Don't* touch me!" she said angrily, slapping my hands away.

"Yeah, you heard the lady. Don't touch her," mocked a voice from the shadows.

Recognizing the speaker, I stiffened up. It was Brent, and from the laughter around us, I realized he wasn't alone. His two friends from the bar were with him. The three stepped around a van, all grinning at me with malevolence in their eyes.

"Go away, Brent," Chloe said, moving closer to me. "Leave us alone."

"It sounds like you need help, Chloe," he said in a mocking voice. "Or are you two role-playing some kind of creepy Krampus fantasy?"

"Fuck off," I replied.

Brent's smile fell. He approached me, a threatening look on his face. "You want to make me?"

"I'd rather not waste my time, but I will if you don't get out of my face. By the way," I smirked, "how did your circle-jerking party behind the van go? Everything come out all right?"

Furious, Brent came at me, fists flying. I quickly blocked him and then took a swing myself, catching him in the face. Before I could get off another punch, his two buddies jumped me and things got ugly.

THIRTY EIGHT

CHLOE

I SCREAMED AS Brent's friends went after Graham. They both started throwing punches, catching him from both sides, not giving Graham much of a chance to fight back.

"Stop it!" I yelled, trying to get between them.

"Dammit, Chloe. Don't be stupid!" Brent snapped. He pulled me away from the fight and tried dragging me to his car while I kicked and screamed for help. I couldn't believe this was happening right out in the open and nobody was around to help.

"Let her go!" Graham hollered, struggling to get away from the other two.

Ignoring him, Brent tried picking me up, but I bit him in the cheek. Screaming in pain, he backhanded me. I stumbled, falling down on the icy pavement and flat on my ass. Crying, I tried crawling away from him, but he wouldn't have it.

Brent touched his cheek. "That fucking hurt, Chloe. You're going to pay for this." He leaned down and grabbed me by the hair. Pulling me up to my feet, he tried getting me into his car again. It was then that the front door of the bar opened up and two people walked out. Recognizing Graham's friend Matt and his wife, I began screaming for their help.

Shocked, Matt reached into his jacket and pulled out a gun. He raced to where Graham was scuffling with Brent's buddies and fired the weapon up into the sky. Shocked, everyone froze.

"Whoa," Brent said, letting me go. He held up his hands and smiled. "Take it easy, man. No need to bring in guns."

Ignoring him, Matt asked Graham if he was okay.

Graham, whose eye was beginning to swell, nodded and then took a swing at the assailant on his left. He must have connected hard, because the man dropped like a ton of bricks. Graham twisted to take a shot at the other guy, but the man was already running away.

Scowling, Graham spit out a wad of blood. "Fucking pussy," he said and turned his sights on Brent.

"Dude, this was a mistake. I'm sorry," Brent said, holding up his hands in defense as Graham approached him.

In answer, Graham pulled him by the jacket and slammed his forehead into Brent's. Shocked, I watched him fall down, unconscious.

"What in the hell was going on out here?" Matt asked, putting his gun away.

"They just jumped us. No reason other than her ex is a dickhead," Graham said, walking over to me. He put his arm around my shoulders affectionately. "Are you okay?"

I was shaking like a leaf, but okay. I nodded.

He pulled me in gently for a hug and I heard him groan in pain.

"I'm so sorry," I said, staring up at Graham's face. He was definitely getting a shiner.

"It's not your fault," he said, wincing as I tried touching his face.

"I know but, I'm still sorry," I replied softly. "We need to get that iced."

Graham bent down and grabbed a handful of snow. He blotted the cold powder onto his face. "There. Good as new."

I snorted.

"Do either of you want me to call the police?" Matt asked.

"No. Honestly, I just want to get the fuck out of here," Graham replied. "By the way, what's with the gun?"

"I have my Carry-And-Conceal," he said.

I sighed. "Thank God for that."

"We should all get out of here before those two come around," Matt said as his wife approached cautiously. He introduced us and then Graham thanked him for helping.

"No problem. I'm just glad I came out here when I did. It looks like he was going to try and kidnap Chloe."

Graham looked at me and smiled. "My girl? Over my dead body."

I looked at him in surprise.

His eyes twinkled.

THIRTY
NINE

GRAHAM

AFTER MATT AND his wife left, Chloe and I got back into my truck. Sitting wasn't the most pleasurable experience either. My ribs were sore from getting tag-teamed.

"Are you sure you're okay?" she asked, studying my face again with concern.

"I'll be fine. It's just a black eye."

"What about your chest and ribs? You gasped a little when you were hugging me."

"They're bruised, but okay."

Her eyes narrowed. "Are you sure? I should take a look at you and make sure there aren't any internal injuries."

"I'm totally fine. They hit me mostly in the face. I've been in worse fights before, Chloe."

The look she gave me told me she believed it.

Noticing Brent getting back up, I started the engine. "Let's just go. I'd like to pound him a new asshole, but I'm not spending another Christmas in jail."

Her eyes softened. "I don't want you to either."

Thinking back to our earlier fight, I sighed. "Are you still angry with me?"

"Damn right I am," she admitted. "I mean, I still can't believe you thought—"

Before she could finish her sentence, I leaned forward and kissed her. Fortunately, she didn't resist and opened her mouth to me. I slid my tongue inside, wanting to taste every inch of her. Finding out Chloe hadn't been with Cleaner was both a relief and a wild aphrodisiac. As much pain as I was in, I still wanted her now more than anything… and planned to.

Regretfully, I pulled away so we could get out of there.

"I still think we should get you checked out," she said, checking her hair in the mirror. I remembered Brent pulling her by it in the parking lot. It had pissed the hell out of me. Her hair was beautiful. Almost like spun gold. Even now I itched to run my fingers through it, but knew she might be in pain.

"I'm fine. How's your head? I wanted to kill him when he grabbed you by the hair."

"I'm fine," she said, putting the visor back up. "It hurt, but not anymore."

I reached over and touched it gently. "Good. The only man who should be pulling you by the hair is me," I said, now running my finger down her cheek. "When I'm inside of you."

Chloe's eyes widened and her cheeks turned a rosy color. I could tell by the look on her face that I'd said something she liked.

"So, what are you waiting for?" she asked, smiling slowly.

Talk about instant wood.

"Yeah, what am I waiting for?" I turned my eyes back onto the road and decided that come hell or high water, I wasn't going to let that invitation slide

FORTY

CHLOE

I WANTED GRAHAM so badly and it was frustrating because the road conditions were still horrible and we were out in the middle of nowhere. Plus, I didn't know how much pain he was really in and didn't want to hurt him.

"Maybe we should wait until you're not so sore," I suggested.

"It's going to hurt more if I have to wait," he replied with a devilish smile. "Believe me."

I smiled back. "Maybe we should find a hotel?"

"I love that idea, but I don't think there are any for several miles."

"Damn," I pouted, biting my lower lip.

He reached over and ran a hand over my thigh. "Don't worry, darlin'. I'll find us something."

His touch sent shivers up and down my leg. Yes, I was still angry with him for thinking I'd had sex with Cleaner, but I was willing to forgive him. After all, I knew he'd been cheated on the previous year and probably had some major trust issues.

After a couple more strokes of his hand on my thigh, he moved it away. "Fuck, I need you naked. I don't know how much longer I can wait. How do you feel about back roads?"

"Depends on if you're talking about mine?" I replied, grinning evilly.

"God, woman… you really are naughtier than you look. I think Santa is going to have to teach you a lesson," he said, adjusting himself while looking at me with wild, hungry eyes.

Just thinking about the implications made the flesh between my legs spasm. "I'm going to hold you to it."

He grinned.

After another half of a mile, Graham turned down a dirt road and we drove until something caught his eye. He slammed on the brakes, barely missing a large deer that hopped into our path. The SUV skidded and suddenly, we were stuck in a ditch.

"Dammit," Graham said, putting the truck in reverse. He tried backing up, but it only made things worse.

"Did you try putting it into 4-Low?" I asked.

"Yes," he snapped. "Of course."

I scowled at him. "You don't have to be so grouchy,"

"I'm not grouchy. I'm just frustrated."

"Well, don't take it out on me."

Growling in the back of his throat, he unbuckled his seatbelt and got out of the SUV.

"Fuck!" he hollered after noticing how bad things were on the outside of the truck.

I rolled down the window. "Should we call for help?"

"We can't. My phone is dead. Remember?" he said, running a hand through his hair. "I'm going to have to walk up the road and see if there's a house nearby with a phone."

"I'll come with you," I said, rolling up the window.

He jumped back into the truck. "You're not going anywhere. Just stay here where it's warm and safe."

"Safe?" I replied, looking outside and into the darkness. "I feel like we're in the scene of a horror movie, and as soon as you leave, I'm going to get murdered. Or, you're going to get killed trying to find help. I'll just sit here waiting and waiting and waiting for you."

"You've been watching too many movies. I'll be back," he said, opening up the door again.

"I'm serious, Graham. I'm not staying here," I said firmly.

He stared at me for a few seconds and then sighed. "Fine. Grab the flashlight from the glove compartment. Please."

"Okay."

IT WAS COLD and of course the snow was deep, making it hard to walk fast. Fortunately, there was an old farmhouse up the road. We walked up and onto the porch.

"This doesn't look very promising," I said, as he knocked on the door. The place actually looked deserted. The lights were out and there weren't any vehicles parked outside. There was a large, old barn, but it was obviously rundown and empty. There was barely even a roof on it.

"Come on," Graham muttered, shivering. All he had on was the Santa outfit and the T-shirt underneath. It certainly wasn't warm enough to protect him very long from the elements. We needed to get him warm.

I reached out and knocked harder.

"I think you're right. Nobody is home," he said, trying the knob. To our surprise, it was open.

"Okay, this is creepy. Maybe we should think about this," I said as he pushed the door open. This was definitely beginning to feel like a scary movie.

"I'm freezing my ass off. We're just going to look for a phone, okay? So, I can call Tank."

I nodded.

He stepped inside first. "Hello?! Anyone home?!"

Spotting a light switch, I tried turning on it on, but there was nothing.

"Well, that's that," he said, sighing. "The electricity isn't working. There's no furniture," he said, staring into the dark living room. "Obviously, the owner of this place isn't going to have a working phone either."

"At least it's warmer in here than out there."

"That's the only good thing."

I let out a ragged sigh. "Let's at least look around and see if there's a landline. Maybe the phone company forgot to turn off the service here and we'll find one somewhere?"

"Your cup is always half full, isn't it?" he asked in amusement.

"Most of the time, yes. I try to stay positive," I replied, walking across the wooden floor, the sound of my boots echoing loudly in the darkness.

"I guess that's pretty commendable on your part," he said. "Especially having dated an asshole like Brent."

"Thanks." I walked into the kitchen first and found that just like the rest of the house, it was empty.

"Anything?" he asked, coming up behind me.

I sighed. "No."

"You know, I guess this isn't *so* bad," he murmured, sliding his arms around my waist. "We're alone. It's dry. And you're so very… hot."

He pushed my hair to the side and blazed a warm trail of his own down the side of my neck with his lips. Closing my eyes, I sighed in pleasure as his hand slid under my sweatshirt, to my breasts. Squeezing them, he groaned his approval.

"Mm… Graham," I whispered, tilting my head back. I could feel his cock pressing against my buttocks as he fondled my breasts. Finding the clasp on my bra, he opened it up and released them.

"I'm going to come just touching you," he said, cupping my bare breasts. Finding my nipples, he squeezed and rolled the nubs between his fingers, creating delightful shockwaves down to my core.

"Yes," I breathed.

Biting my earlobe he lowered his hand to my jeans and unbuttoned them again. "Let's try this again," he whispered, unzipping them.

Anticipating his touch, I froze as his fingers slid down the front of my panties and he touched my mound.

"Fuck," he growled, finding my clit. "You're so wet."

Gasping in pleasure, I whimpered and moaned as he fingered me, one hand on my breast, the other down below, strumming. Within seconds, he brought me to orgasm.

"God, I'd love to just bend you over the counter and fuck this pretty, wet pussy of yours," he said, sticking his finger inside me, moving in and out. "But, I think I want to see you come for me again first."

Closing my eyes I began to moan again, wishing it was his cock inside of me. I began begging him for it.

"Patience." Graham removed his hand and turned me around. Staring at me with hot, burning lust, he pulled off my sweatshirt and pushed the bra away from my shoulders, letting it fall to the floor.

"Beautiful," he whispered, grabbing both my breasts in the palms of his hands. Lowering his warm mouth, he took one nipple into his mouth, and then the other, rolling and sucking the nubs, making love to my breasts until he decided he wanted more.

"Take off your pants," he said, stepping back.

I took the boots off first and then the jeans, meanwhile watching him remove the Santa suit. Soon, he was standing in front of me, wearing nothing but a pair of black Jockeys. The moon shined through the kitchen window, over his muscular chest and arms. There didn't seem to be much bruising, which was a relief. Just pure, male sexiness. If that wasn't eye candy enough, the hard outline of his cock made my mouth water.

"Put your boots back on," he ordered, his voice husky.

I did what he asked while he watched, fucking me with his eyes.

"Damn," he said, after I zipped up my boots and stood up straight. He moved in front of me and grabbed a hold of my panties. "I like these, but they're in the way," he said, ripping them off of me.

FORTY ONE

GRAHAM

S HE WAS SO gorgeous and sexy, I could barely control myself. After ripping off her panties, I wanted to bury my cock deep inside of her tight pussy, but I wasn't going to last. I wanted her to come again before I did. That was going to be challenging enough. Seeing her there, in all of her naked glory, was enough to drive a man insane. Round, heavy tits, a small waist, and a curvy ass that I wanted to sink my teeth into. And so help me, before the night was over, I would.

Picking her up by the waist, I set her down on the counter and pushed her legs apart. Seeing her naked, with nothing but her heeled boots on, was making my dick pulsate.

"Graham," Chloe said, reaching toward my underwear. "Let me touch you. Please."

"You're going to have to wait," I said slapping her fingers away. As much as I wanted to feel her hand wrapped around my woody, I had other plans.

"Maybe I should make you wait then," she said, with a little grin.

I ran my hand over her breasts, down to her stomach, all the way to her mound, leaving a trail of goosebumps.

She shivered.

I stared at her rock-hard nipples. "I could take a picture of you and never stop looking at it," I said, admiring her beauty. The light from the moon shimmered over her skin. I'd never seen anything so sexy or tempting in my life.

"Too bad your phone is dead. Maybe I'd let you take one. But, only if you let me see your cock."

"Fine. Look but don't touch," I said, lowering my underwear. My angry, neglected cock sprang up, the tip moist with pre-cum.

"Oh, God," she moaned, staring at it hungrily. "Fuck me, Graham."

"Say that again," I said, stroking it lightly.

Her eyes were half-closed as she stared at my cock. "Fuck me, Graham. I want to feel you inside me."

Wanting so many things myself, I leaned down, buried my face between her thighs and tasted her honey first.

FORTY TWO

CHLOE

I GASPED IN pleasure when he found my clit and began teasing it. Unlike Brent, the only other guy who'd given me oral sex, Graham used the perfect amount of pressure, keeping it steady as he flicked back and forth with his tongue.

"Mm... Graham," I whimpered.

He slid a finger in, and then two, rubbing my G-spot and creating a pressure from within while his tongue danced in other places. Moaning, I squirmed and pushed against his face.

"That's it, baby," he whispered between licks. Wiggling his nose he growled. "Come for Graham."

Arching my back, I screamed out his name as I exploded into a deep orgasm, one so powerful that it made me laugh and cry at the same time.

Graham kissed both my inner thighs and then stood up. He held me against his chest while I calmed down and pulled myself together.

"You okay?" he asked, running his fingers through my hair.

"Better than okay."

"Good. Because we're not done." He released me and I hopped off the counter.

"I should hope we're not, Graham," I said, reaching into his underwear. I grabbed his cock and he groaned in pleasure.

"I had no idea you were hiding this beast," I teased, stroking around the tip.

Chuckling, Graham pushed my hand away again. "I'm not going to last, especially if you keep doing that," he said, reaching for his wallet. He opened it up and pulled out a condom.

"Then, we'll do it again," I replied, watching as he tore open the package. "Wait."

He looked at me.

I grabbed his cock again and wrapped my lips around it. He was big, which excited me even more. I couldn't wait to feel him down below, but watching his face was erotically hypnotic.

Graham moaned as I sucked and stroked his shaft. His skin was smooth and salty from pre-cum, his cock, thick, hard, and demanding release. When the sensations of my tongue and mouth became too much for him, he pushed me away and slid the condom on.

"How do you want it?" he asked, looking around the kitchen. "There really isn't a comfortable spot in here."

I turned around and leaned over the counter. Looking back at him over my shoulder, I gave him an answer.

175

His eyes smoldered with desire. Grabbing me around the waist, he positioned himself for the best angle, and began pushing his cock inside of me.

"Oh, yeah," I gasped, feeling him slowly enter and fill me up. I hadn't had a man inside of me for so long, and this guy was packing so much girth, I didn't know if he could even fit all the way in.

"Fuck," he whispered, still trying to push further.

I leaned down a little more and suddenly… we were as one.

FORTY THREE

GRAHAM

I WAS IN pussy heaven. She was so tight and wet, it was hard to stay focused. Especially seeing her bent over. I pulled out as much as I dared and then plunged back in, enjoying the sounds she was making and the way her cunt grappled my cock. Soon, I was thrusting in and out, one hand on her jiggling tits, the other holding her in place as I banged her. I tried to hold off as long as I could, but she was so warm, wet, and tight, it was impossible. A few more thrusts and I was shooting my load, gasping from the ecstasy as I rammed into her a couple more times.

"That was incredible," Chloe said breathlessly.

"You're telling me. I'm sorry," I said in a ragged voice, pulling out. "I know it didn't last very long…"

"You have *nothing* to be sorry about," she said, looking back at me. "I've never been fucked like that before. Ever."

I grinned. "Really?"

"Everything you did… everything… I'm still shaking."

I noticed her legs were trembling, but I'd thought it was from the coolness in the air. Now that I was spent, I could feel a draft coming into the kitchen.

Staring down at her heart-shaped ass, I told her it had blown my mind, too.

"I don't think I've ever come so hard in my life," I said, dropping the condom into the sink. I leaned down and bit her in the ass playfully. Just like I'd been wanting to do.

She squealed.

I kissed the pink spot. "We have all night. And tomorrow. And the day after that."

"So, this isn't like a 'Cleaner' type of thing?" she asked, shyly.

"What? Hell, no." I turned her around and pulled her into my arms. "Chloe. This is an 'us' kind of thing. Now that I've had you, I can't imagine letting you go."

Her eyebrow arched. "Are you sure? You're not just saying that because we're in the middle of nowhere? I mean, I've heard about the lifestyle biker club members have. I know about the club whores and the parties."

"I like to party, but I'm not into club whores. You can ask anyone in the club." I nuzzled her neck. "I'm into women who with substance. You, my sweet Chloe, have everything I could possibly need."

"Are you sure? We barely know each other. What if I'm not the woman you think I am?" she asked, staring up at me curiously.

I stared down into her eyes and was touched by the concern reflected in them. It was an honest question and she deserved a straight answer.

"My heart says that you are. Even if I'm wrong, which I highly doubt, it will be worth finding out."

She smiled.

"So, what do you say, Chloe? Do you want to spend Christmas with me?"

"More than anything."

I kissed her on the lips, my heart already belonging to her. I only hoped I hadn't fucked everything up with my quick-to-judge attitude. She deserved more than that and we both deserved happiness. I only hoped I could give her what she needed and wanted. And unlike Bonnie, it would be enough...

FORTY FOUR

CHLOE

One Year Later…

"GRAHAM, STOP IT," I said, smacking his hand away from my breasts. We were just leaving the nursing home he'd visited the year before; he'd played Santa again and I'd dressed up as his elf assistant. Although the Gold Vipers had selected a different retirement home this year to visit, this one held a special place in Graham's heart. So, we'd stopped at the dollar store and purchased a bunch of small gifts for the residents. They'd been so grateful and sweet. I could see why Graham wanted to make it an annual tradition.

"I can't help it," he said, pulling me close. "I got all worked up in there watching you walk around in the elf suit."

This year, Graham had picked out one for me and it was almost as bad as the sexy one Tank had ordered the year before in error. The only reason I'd worn it to the nursing home was that it came with a jacket that covered the bodice. My breasts were not in the least bit on display, but Graham still couldn't keep his horny hands off of me. Normally I didn't mind, but we'd just walked out of a nursing home and, to my horror, he'd given Ed, a resident, a blow-up doll. The deaf old man had been ecstatic, and in fact had disappeared to his room shortly after.

"I still can't believe you gave that man a sex doll," I said, shaking my head, but smiling. "What were you thinking?"

"He asked Santa for one last year. He had to deliver. Speaking of deliveries," he said, taking my hand and placing it on his rising cock. "I have a special package with your name on it."

I gently pushed him away. As much as I wanted to open up that gift, I had something for him.

"You're no fun," he said, as we approached his SUV.

"Quit pouting, Santa," I said.

His lip went down like a petulant child and I began to sing the words to "Santa Claus Is Coming To Town."

He grinned. "Speaking of *coming* to town," he said, wiggling his eyebrows. "I think Santa needs to pay a visit to yours. Unless you want to come to my North Pole instead?"

"Happily. When we get out of here and back home," I said, getting into the SUV.

Still smiling, Graham got inside and started the engine.

"You know, there aren't very many couples living there," I said, looking over at the nursing home. "It's kind of sad."

"You mean married couples?"

I nodded.

He sighed. "Yeah. It gets pretty lonely for some of them not having a partner."

I looked back at him. "Wouldn't it be nice if we lived long enough to be together in something like that?"

"I hope I never have to," he replied. "Live in one, I mean. They're sad."

"Sometimes you have no choice," I said. "Which is why I think we should start planning ahead. For our future."

"What do you mean? Start up a retirement fund?"

I held back my smile. In the last year, so much had happened. For one, Graham and I had fallen deeply in love. It hadn't taken long, especially with there being so much passion between us. In the summer, we'd even purchased a house together and I'd talked him into letting me get another dog from one of the shelters. It was a mutt, but an adorable one who loved his new family. His name was Vinnie and Graham spoiled the hell out of him.

For two, Kai had kicked Trey to the curb and was now dating a professional basketball player. Apparently, he had gotten sick of Trey's freeloading and just kicked him out one day.

And finally, Graham was now a fully patched Gold Viper, which couldn't have made him happier. He'd also taken a DNA test, along with Raptor, and it was confirmed that they were more than likely brothers. Interestingly enough, Jordan refused to take the test. Jessica said it had something to do with a previous occupation, which she wasn't allowed to discuss.

Talk about intriguing.

Even Graham had no idea what it was all about.

Feeling nervous suddenly, I pulled a small package out of my pocket and handed it to Graham.

"What is this?" he asked, his eyebrows knitting together.

"Open it."

He tore open the red wrapping paper, and inside was a box with a diamond and gold ring. Graham looked at me, not understanding, which I'd expected. He'd approached me with the subject of getting married last summer and I'd brushed it off. The truth was, I'd wanted to ask him so he'd understand how truly I loved the man. Bonnie's cheating had left Graham insecure and I wanted him to realize that there was absolutely no reason for it. He was everything to me and all I would ever want.

I took his hand and told him how much I loved him.

"I love you, too," he said, searching my eyes.

"I know you brought up the subject of marriage already. I didn't sound very interested, but," I smiled, "I wanted to be the one to ask you. Even then."

He looked surprised.

Being the emotional woman I was, my eyes filled with tears. "I know you love me. I can feel it every time you look at me. Every word you say and everything you do is an affirmation of how big your heart is. I want you to know there will never be anyone else for me. *Ever.* I want you to be the father to my children. I want to grow old with you, and if we end up in a nursing home, I want us to be together."

"So, what you're saying is that we absolutely, positively *have* to have children?" he asked, smiling.

I groaned. He was always teasing me about not wanting any. But, I knew he did. "Yes. That's nonnegotiable."

"Fine," he said, chuckling as he pulled out a small package from his Santa suit. He handed it to me. "Curiously enough, I was going to ask you the same thing. Only, tomorrow. Merry Christmas."

"Hold up. You haven't answered me yet," I said seriously, nodding toward the ring I'd spent hours picking out. Adriana, who owned a jewelry store with her mother Vanda, had helped me look through dozens of rings.

Chuckling, he took it out of the box and slipped it onto his finger. "Yes, Chloe, I will definitely marry you. Hell, I'd marry you right now if I had the chance."

"Thank you." I leaned over and kissed him.

"Now, open yours," he said.

I ripped the packaging off and opened up the ring box. It was a sparkly diamond solitaire and everything I could have ever wanted. Smiling, I slipped it onto my finger and kissed him again. "It's beautiful. Thank you."

He glanced down at his ring. "You did a fine job of picking this one out, too. I'm not much for jewelry, but I'll wear this."

"You're damn right you will," I teased. "That's nonnegotiable either. I don't care what kind of rules the Gold Vipers have, you're wearing my ring."

"Back to having children." He tapped the front of my costume. "Since we're going to make it legal, I say we start making a brood of little elves to help us with the holidays."

"A brood?" I asked. "How many?"

He started driving out of the parking lot. "As many as it takes. The more the merrier, right? Ho, ho, ho. He, he, he."

I chuckled. "You really have found your Christmas spirit, haven't you?"

He grabbed my hand. "No. Something much more important."

I smiled. "Me?"

He turned on some Christmas music. "I was going to say the last blow-up doll at *Sex World* for old Ed. Do you know how hard those things are to find?"

Gasping, I slugged him in the shoulder and we both started laughing.

The End

CPSIA information can be obtained
at www.ICGtesting.com
Printed in the USA
BVHW040851111021
618669BV00018B/578